Ever After High™

The Storybook of Legends

Ever After High™

The Storybook of Legends

BY SHANNON HALE

LITTLE, BROWN AND COMPANY

New York   Boston

Little, Brown and Company
Hachette Book Group
1290 Avenue of the Americas, New York, NY 10104
Visit us at LBYR.com
everafterhigh.com
monsterhigh.com

Originally published in hardcover and ebook by
Little, Brown and Company in October 2013

First Paperback Edition: September 2017

Little, Brown and Company is a division of Hachette Book Group, Inc.
The Little, Brown name and logo are trademarks of Hachette Book Group, Inc.

The publisher is not responsible for websites (or their content)
that are not owned by the publisher.

Library of Congress Control Number 2013024496

ISBN: 978-0-316-40125-8 (pbk.)

Printed in the United States of America

LSC-C

For Dean, my Happily Ever After

CONTENTS

A Very Short PROLOGUE

THE GREAT HALL OF EVER AFTER HIGH smelled like floor wax and old stone mixed with the tangy musk of magic. The fire in the hearth burned blue. An enchanted frog sat beside the arched doorway, repeating, "Welcome to the Legacy Day ceremony. Please watch your step. *Crrrroak*."

The second-year students passed the frog—some tripping on the step—and walked solemnly outside. On the castle terrace, the audience waited in gilded chairs. Beyond a stream-carved ravine, the Enchanted

Forest twinkled with the bright trails of fairies. But the students hadn't gathered on the terrace for the view. All eyes were on Headmaster Grimm, standing at the podium. He smoothed down his gray-turning-white hair and smiled at the audience.

He held up the Storybook of Legends so all could see. Magic sparked off its gold-embossed cover like glitter in a whirlwind.

"Today is the most important day at Ever After High—indeed, the most important day in all of the Land of Ever After."

The audience cheered.

"This year, Legacy Day is *your* day," the headmaster said to the second-year students, who were lined up before the stairs to the podium. They were dressed in their formal Legacy Day outfits—beautiful ball gowns, regal prince suits, mermaid dresses dripping salty puddles.

"Today you take the first step in claiming your glorious fairytale legacies. Once you sign the Storybook of Legends, you are magically bound to your parent's story. You *will* relive it. In this way, your story, your legacy—and your very life—will be preserved."

The headmaster placed the book carefully on the podium and stepped back.

The first student to climb the stairs rode on the back of a mouse all the way up the side of the podium. The tiny boy leaped off the mouse and declared his destiny as the next Tom Thumb. His signature in the book was a blot the size of an ant.

The daughter of a fairy godmother pushed her glasses up her nose and signed her promise to become the next Cinderella's helper.

A future witch wore her mother's black dress and pointy hat, but lavender flip-flops peeked from beneath the ragged hem. She signed with a frown, hastily wiping a tear off her cheek.

While everyone watched with interest, two in the audience barely breathed. They barely blinked. One leaned forward, yearning for her chance to sign. The other leaned back, as if nervous to get too close.

Both would take their turn at the book in just one year. And one's choice would change the Land of Ever After forever. After.

CHAPTER 1

NEVER TOUCH THE MIRROR

ONCE UPON A NEW SCHOOL YEAR, RAVEN Queen was packing. She blasted Tailor Quick's new album from her MirrorPod, dancing while grabbing things from her closet and tossing them into her clothing trunk. The heap of clothes was entirely purple and black, so she threw in a pair of silver sandals to add color.

Raven opened her window. The sun was setting into the copper sea. The last page of summer was closing.

"Hey, Ooglot!" she called out as she hefted her trunk onto the windowsill of her fourth-story bedroom. She let the trunk fall. In the courtyard below, the family ogre caught it with one blue hand and waved to her. She waved back.

Summer had been nice. No homework—just hours and hours to listen to music and read adventure novels. A couple of days each week she had babysat Cook's twin boys—Butternut and Pie—in exchange for heaps of pastries. And she and Dad had sailed their little boat down the coast to spend a week with Pinocchio and his daughter, Cedar Wood. Raven had loved making tea visits with the Blue-Haired Fairy, playing card games by the fire, and staying up late with Cedar, singing karaoke and laughing into their pillows.

All nice as mice. But Raven was eager to rejoin her friends at Ever After High for her second year of boarding school.

She was trying very hard not to think about how her Legacy Day was just a few weeks away. Ever since witnessing Legacy Day as a first-year, she'd done her best to block it out. Back then, the future had seemed so distant.

A foghorn bellowed, calling her to dinner.

Raven put on a sweater as she left her room.

Queen Castle was chilly. There were far too many unoccupied rooms to bother lighting fires in all their hearths. When her mother had ruled, the castle had teemed with servants, soldiers, and creatures of the shadows. And all of them had watched young Raven, ready to tattle to her mother if they caught Raven doing anything kind.

"Raven," her mother would say, "Yop the Goblin heard you apologize to a rat for stepping on its tail. Such behavior must stop!"

"But I didn't mean to step on its tail," she'd say.

"Not that. The apology! The Evil Queen never apologizes for anything. You must learn that now."

Raven preferred the castle mostly empty.

She made her way through the massive Great Hall, feeling as if she'd been swallowed by a whale. She stuck out her tongue at the shadows and slid down the banister of the staircase as she used to when she was a kid.

She flung open the huge dining room doors and announced, "I'm here!" Years ago her mother hosted hundreds of guests at that dining table. Tonight, as usual, the only diners were Raven, her father, Cook, and Cook's four-year-old sons.

"Raven!" Butternut and Pie said in unison. They had hair as orange as Butternut's namesake and faces as round as Pie's.

"Hey, little Cooklings," she said.

"I made this for you," said Pie, pushing a piece of paper across the table. Raven held up a finger painting of herself done in all black and purple.

"Wicked cool. Thank you," she said.

Raven's father, the Good King, kissed her forehead when she sat beside him. His trimmed beard was beginning to gray, and the top of his head was totally bald, as if his hair had made room for the golden crown he rarely bothered to wear. His eyes were bright blue and brightened even more when he smiled—which was often.

"All packed?" he asked. "Don't forget a warm coat. And rain boots. And an enchanted umbrella."

"Got it," said Raven. "And don't you stay cooped up in here all year without me. Cook, make sure he gets outside, goes sailing and fishing."

"Of course. Now dinner. I made roast duck," Cook said hopefully, lifting the platter.

"I'll just have a princess pea–butter sandwich,

please," Raven said while playing peekaboo behind her napkin with Butternut.

Cook rolled her eyes but handed Raven her usual sandwich.

"Thank you," Raven said, and then winced automatically. But her mother wasn't there to scold her for being nice.

Her father must have noticed her wince, because he put a comforting hand on her shoulder and smiled.

"My meat is cold," said Butternut.

"I can warm it up for you," Raven said, wiggling her fingers as if preparing to cast a spell.

"No!" both Cook and the king said at once, lunging to their feet.

Raven laughed.

"Oh my, you had me for a moment." The king pressed his hand to his heart and sat back down.

A couple of years before, Raven had tried to reheat her father's meal and ended up setting the entire table on fire. She wouldn't make that mistake again. Dark magic + good intentions = catastrophe.

After the plum pudding, the Good King said, "Cook, thank you so much for a perfect dinner.

Raven, would you...?" He inclined his head toward the door.

Raven's stomach turned cold, but she followed him out.

Once they were alone in the hall, he whispered, "It's time, Raven. If you'd rather not..."

"No, I'll go talk to her."

"I'll go with you," he said.

Raven shook her head. She was fifteen now. She was old enough to face her mother alone.

Raven straightened her shoulders and began the long walk to the Queen's Wing in the Other Side of the Castle for the first time in a year. Colors dimmed—dark wood walls, scarlet and black carpets. Portrait paintings looked down. Her mother smiling. Her mother not smiling. Her mother's profile. A close-up of her mother's nose. In one, her mother was winking. In all of them, she was beautiful.

Monstrous statues seemed to watch Raven as she passed. Drapes rustled where there was no draft. Raven's forehead prickled with cold sweat.

Two guards in shiny armor stood outside her mother's old bedroom, wielding spiky spears and magic staffs. They nodded to her as she opened the door.

"Remember," said one, "never touch the mirror."

"I remember," she said.

The room was so thick with cobwebs it seemed as if skeletons had decorated for a party. Raven fought her way through the webs to the far wall and ripped the velvet cloth off the mirror. She saw her own reflection staring back—long black hair with purple highlights, dark eyebrows, strong nose and chin. It was strange to see her own face. She usually avoided looking at herself in mirrors. Mirror-gazing had been her mother's hobby.

"Mirror, mirror on the wall," she said, "um...show me my mother."

The mirror didn't require a rhyme to work. Rhyming was *so* last chapter.

The mirror sparked, electricity skating across its silver surface. Slowly her mother appeared. She was wearing a striped jumpsuit. Her dark hair was piled on her head in the shape of a crown.

"Raven, is that you? You're so...so beautiful!" The Evil Queen laughed. "You *are* going to give that fair-skinned, blood-lipped brat a run for her money!"

Raven pulled her hair out from behind her ear, letting it fall over half her face.

"Hey, Mother," she said. "How's, you know, mirror prison?"

"Meh," the Evil Queen said with a pretty shrug. "Tell me all the gossip. What's happening in Ever After? Did they figure out how to undo my poisoning of Wonderland madness yet? Has someone else copied me and tried to take over all the kingdoms? Is your father still a mind-numbing excuse for a man?"

Raven clenched her fists. *Don't make fun of my dad!* she wanted to shout. But she met those dark eyes in the mirror, took a deep breath, and looked down. Even with her mother imprisoned far away, she didn't dare argue back. "Everything's pretty much the same as last year. And the year before."

"Ha! See what happens when I'm gone? *Nothing.* I made life interesting. I hope you learn from this, darling. You have to go out there and force life to be what you want it to be, like I did."

"Yeah," said Raven. Her mother had certainly made her childhood interesting. In those days, the castle was always crowded with soldiers in spiked armor and creatures that scurried through shadows and hissed at her. Quality time with Mother had included sitting on her lap while the queen met with her generals and hatched plots to kill, conquer, and rule, or spending hours in the dungeon workshop, coughing on smoke and helping Mother make toxic potions and evil spells.

"So are you ready for your Legacy Year?" asked the queen. "Ready to sign the Storybook of Legends and bind yourself to following in my footsteps?"

Raven shrugged.

"You should be eager to become the next Evil Queen. Why, your legacy is one of power, control, and command! Just think, you could have been born to one of those pathetic princesses who have to sit in a tower and wait to be rescued. Or worse, get suckered into eating a poisoned apple."

The queen cackled beautifully. If ever a cackle could bring a tear to your eye, it was the Evil Queen's.

"I guess I just...I just..."

"What? Don't mumble. Stop slouching and speak up like a Queen. Now, what were you saying?"

Raven straightened her spine. "Nothing. Never mind."

"Don't be so timid, Raven. This is your chance to show those dull 'good' folk just what you're made of!"

"Okay, I'll try." And as a show of effort, she cracked a small smile.

"I'm so proud! Oh, I miss you, my beautiful baby girl." Her mother lifted her hand, pressing it against the mirror as if she were just on the other side of a window. "Let me touch you, even if it's only through glass."

Raven's hand lifted, almost of its own accord. Her mother really did love her, in her way. Hope was like a sticky, too-sweet syrup she yearned to drink just one more time. But Raven stopped her hand before she touched the mirror. This wasn't the actual mirror prison. That was far away and locked up tight. But her mother was such a powerful sorceress, she might be able to take Raven's hand even through a viewing portal.

"I love you, Mother," said Raven, "but I'm not helping you escape."

The queen's eyes narrowed, and her hand dropped. "*Hmph.* If you were as evil as I raised you to be, you wouldn't hesitate. I must say, Raven Queen, I'm disappointed in you. Never mind. I'll watch with interest to see what you accomplish. You have inherited a bottomless capacity for true evil and breathtaking power. Don't waste it." She leaned so close all Raven could see in the mirror were her mother's deep purple eyes. "Give 'em hex, Raven."

Raven swallowed. All she wanted was to run away.

Their time ended and the mirror turned off. Instead of her mother's face, Raven saw her own again. It was remarkable, really, how much they looked alike.

CHAPTER 2

SIMPLY, UNQUESTIONABLY PERFECT

APPLE WHITE OPENED THE PINK SILK curtains even wider to let in all that buttery sunshine.

"My, what a perfect day for travel!" she said.

Her bedroom was bustling with servants in matching white uniforms, dwarves running errands, and friendly woodland creatures.

A robin hovered before Apple, a red slipper in its beak. It cocked its head to one side as if asking a question.

"Yes, pack that one," said Apple. "In fact, let's just pack all my shoes, shall we?"

The squirrels rustling across the floor squeaked in unison. They began carrying shoes from the closet and depositing them in an open trunk as if storing nuts for the winter.

"Not the blue ones," Apple called to a bluebird in her sock drawer. "The white ones, if you please!"

Apple's MirrorPhone played a measure of One Reflection's single "You Don't Know You're Charming" to announce she'd received another hext message. This one was from Briar Beauty. Apple typed with one hand while brushing her blond curls with the other. Her hair never seemed to need brushing, but she was an overachiever.

BRIAR: Apple! When will you get to Ever After High?

APPLE: My father is prepping the Hybrid Carriage now. I should be there in a few short hours.

BRIAR: Hexcellent. Am planning a Book-to-School party. Going to be a page ripper!!!

APPLE: I'm there. Charm you later!

"Snoozy! Snappy!" Apple called to her dwarf lackeys. "The first four trunks are ready to go. Would you be so kind as to carry them down? You too, Pouty—don't you stick out that bottom lip, you silly."

"My name's not Pouty," Frank said poutily.

"Careful with that end, Sloppy!" Apple said cheerily.

"My name is Phil," Sloppy grumbled.

Apple laughed. "You sillies!"

She patted their heads, and they couldn't help but smile. Who could hold back a smile when looking at Apple White?

The sounds of cheering floated in through her window. Apple stepped onto her balcony, and the cheering grew louder. In the courtyard below, hundreds of men, women, and children from the village had gathered, many wearing I ♥ APPLE T-shirts.

"My dear subjects, you are simply, unquestionably perfect!" she called out, tossing candy and coins to the crowd. She kept a candy-and-coin basket on the balcony so she would be ready for adoring crowds at a moment's notice.

"No, *you* are perfect!" someone shouted, and the cheering renewed.

She pressed her hand to her heart. The whole world was so perfectly splendid she could just burst!

Above Apple, some birds carried a long pink ribbon in their beaks. A message was stitched across the satin ribbon: WE LOVE YOU, APPLE! EMBRACE YOUR DESTINY!

Destiny. She was beginning her Legacy Year, the first step in the journey to achieve her own Happily Ever After. Apple could hardly wait.

Apple strode down to the courtyard, where her parents waited like a portrait of the ideal king and queen. Her mother's black hair was curled under her golden crown. Her skin was still white as snow, her lips red as blood. She was as beautiful now as she had been when a magic mirror had named her the Fairest One of All.

Apple's father stood beside his wife, one hand on his sword hilt, always ready to do battle—though, of course, he'd never actually done any battle. His claim to fame had been falling in love with a comatose girl inside a glass coffin. But he looked so regal with a sword.

"This is a royally important year," said her mother as she helped Apple into the Hybrid Carriage. Her voice was high and a little squeaky, as if all that time spent lost in the woods with squirrels had taken its toll. "I am so proud of you. I know you will prepare yourself to be the perfect Snow White."

The maids, servants, guards, and dwarves in the huge Hybrid Carriage all nodded. Apple blushed. They must have noticed how dedicated she was to her subjects, how hard she had been studying Kingdom Management, all the time she put into preparing to be a queen—

"Just look at her eyes, her skin," whispered one of her maids.

"I did not think it possible," a groomsman whispered back, "but she is becoming even more beautiful than her mother."

"So beautiful," said a manservant. "The *perfect* Snow White."

"Well, except for the hair. A shame she was born blond."

Apple winced.

"I think her blond hair is even lovelier than her mother's black hair."

"How can you? The fairytale specifies 'hair like ebony'—"

"Listen, the hair doesn't matter. Her eyes, her nose, those lips, that profile! She is the definition of beauty."

Apple turned her face to the window as the Hybrid Carriage started on its way. Was that all everyone saw in her? A perfect profile? A beauty like her mother? Surely being Snow White meant more than just looking pretty and having black hair.

Legacy Year would be *her* year. The beginning to her story. But she didn't just want to prove that she was pretty enough to be a queen, black hair or blond. She wanted to prove she could rule like one.

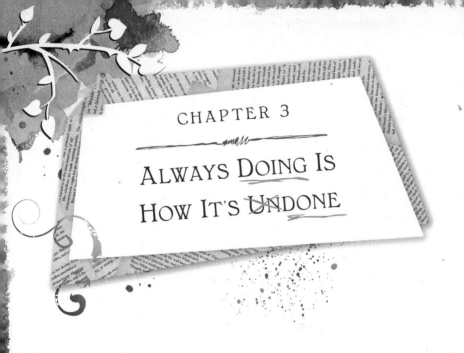

CHAPTER 3

ALWAYS DOING IS
HOW IT'S ~~UNDONE~~

RAVEN HUGGED HER FATHER ONE LAST time, stepped into a Travel Mirror in the front room, and fell out of a Travel Mirror on a high balcony of Ever After High.

Raven peeled herself off the ground, her head swimming, her limbs shaking. She grabbed a banister to keep from falling again. Journey by mirror felt like being rolled into a blanket and tossed into a cold bath. But when your home is a faraway castle clinging to a craggy cliff over a wind-tossed sea, no travel options were convenient.

Ever After High held court on a hill in the center of a valley, its tower-set banners fluttering in the wind like birthday-candle flames. Below her, Raven could see the Village of Book End, and beyond that, pastures, forests, and mountains ranged out to all the fairytale kingdoms.

She took an uneasy step and almost squished a mouse, which scurried out of her way.

"Excuse me," said Raven.

It turned around, shaking a little gray fist at her, then, seeming to recognize her, squeaked and ran off.

Raven frowned.

Her trunk pushed through the mirror after her, landing with a *thunk* on the floor. She pulled on the strap, making slow, grating progress toward the castle door.

The Three Little Pigs were passing by, carrying their clothes tied up in handkerchiefs on the end of poles.

"Hey, would you mind helping me get this trunk up to the dorms?" she asked.

The Pigs turned around with smiles on their round faces, but when they saw Raven, the smiles disappeared. They squealed and hurried away, their trotters clacking on the tiles.

Raven frowned again. All through nursery-rhyme school, other kids had made fun of her for being the Evil Queen's daughter, but she wasn't used to *causing* fear. Her mother had warned her that would happen as she grew older. Well, from her mother it hadn't been phrased as a warning so much as a delightful promise: "Why, one day, the very sight of you will cause all living creatures to shake in terror!"

Ugh.

With her eyes closed and fingers crossed, Raven tried a levitation spell on her trunk. It worked! Sort of. She climbed the stairs to the dorms, her trunk bumping and scraping along behind her, leaving a shiny trail like a snail's slime. She'd have to clean that up later. A couple of times the trunk nudged her in the back, knocking her onto her knees.

She found a door marked RAVEN QUEEN & MADELINE HATTER and would have shouted with delight if she hadn't been so mirror-sick. Rooming with her best friend forever after. What a spell of fortune!

Dizzy, chilly, and beat, Raven collapsed on her bed.

She rolled over, sensing a pea under the mattress. Typical Orientation Week prank. She dug around, found the pea, and tossed it across the room.

A knock at the door. Probably Maddie. She could just walk in, but the girl loved to knock.

Raven pulled herself up and stumbled to the door.

"Mirror travel," she moaned. "I feel like a grape squeezed for juice. Please make me laugh."

She opened the door.

"Laugh?" said a melodious voice that belonged to Apple White, not Madeline Hatter. "I need to work on my humor studies. A queen should be skilled in all subjects."

"Oh! Hey, Apple," she said. "Sorry, I thought you were Maddie."

Apple smiled kindly, her round cheeks pressing with dimples. She was wearing a white top with a flouncy red skirt that celebrated her curvy figure and high-heeled sandals with apple buckles.

The pale princess's presence made Raven aware of her own slouching shoulders and scuffed boots and the way her hairs refused to lie in the same direction. She tried to stand up straight but, by comparison, felt too tall and a bit gaunt.

aring yourself to her, Raven scolded her- *... probably what turned Mother evil in the first ...ce.*

"Hello, Raven! As president of the Royal Student Council, I am personally welcoming every student back to Ever After High."

"Okay, thanks."

Apple stood there as if waiting to be invited in. Raven hesitated. Though they'd never been close, Apple had always been kind to Raven, even back in nursery-rhyme school. Really, Apple was kind to everyone. But hanging out with the girl Raven was destined to poison was a bit awkward.

"So, Legacy Year, huh?" said Raven. *Best. Conversation. Starter. Ever.* Raven sighed at herself.

"Yes, it should be memorable," said Apple.

Raven still had her purse over her shoulder. "Oh, hey, are you hungry? Cook always packs me enough travel snacks for a quest through the Dark Forest." Raven pulled out granola bars, an entire wheel of wax-coated cheese, bread still hot, fruit—

"Ooh, are you going to eat that Golden Delicious?" asked Apple.

"No, it's yours." Raven held out the yellow fruit.

Apple raised one eyebrow. "Jumping ahead in our story a bit, aren't we?"

Raven pulled back the apple, sputtering, "Whoa, it's not—I mean—it's just—"

Apple grinned, and they both laughed.

Raven tossed her the apple. "It's not poisoned, I swear."

"Sure, that's what they all say." Apple rubbed her namesake fruit on her red quilted skirt and bit in, her eyes closing as she crunched. Juice dripped down her perfect chin. "Soooo good." She smiled at Raven, chewing thoughtfully. "I'm not afraid, you know. Of what you'll do. What *we'll* do."

"I know," Raven said. *But I am*, she thought. *I'm terrified.*

"Apple!" Briar Beauty rushed down the hall and gave Apple a bouncing hug. Despite already being one of the tallest girls in their class, Briar always wore super-high heels. Today she wore calf-high boots, a hot-pink minidress, chunky jewelry made of rough-cut stones, as well as her ever-present crownglasses—sunglasses that worked as a crown and held back her long brown hair. Next to Briar's elegant brown skin, Apple seemed even paler.

"You look mesmerizing!" Briar said to Apple. "I love those clever little bows on your sleeves. Summer was so long, wasn't it? But now you're here and we're going to have a Ball! Literally. After the headmaster's orientation stuff in the Charmitorium, we should totally hit the Village Mall and shop for my Book-to-School party. Oh. Hi, Raven."

"Hi, Briar," said Raven.

With another "squee!" Briar pulled Apple away.

Raven shut the door and lay back down on her bed.

There was a *crack* and a puff of dust, and Madeline Hatter came tumbling straight through the wall. She landed with splayed legs on Raven's bed.

"Maddie! What—how did you *do* that?"

"Well, it started as a somersault toward the wall, and I guess I went right through, though I'm not sure I could do that again. But I wish I could because doors can be so boring, can't they? But going *through* the wall is just so…so…*much*!" Maddie brushed off her striped dress and her mint-green-and-lavender hair. Puffs of stone-wall dust billowed around her.

Raven nodded. "I have some serious magic envy. My dark sorcery is…" She shuddered. "But your Wonderland madness is…is—"

"Wonderlandiful! Everyone should be mad, mad, mad."

Raven laughed. "Maddie, you did it. You made me laugh. Thank you!"

"I don't know what I did," Maddie said, "but I suppose that's what comes from always doing—which I *am* always doing—because when one is always doing, one can't help having *done*, can one?"

Raven helped Maddie bring in her things from the hall—using the door this time. Her "things" consisted of a snake charmer's basket full of clothes, sixteen hatboxes, and a tea table already set with cloth, teacups, scones and jam, and a steaming pot of rose hip tea.

Maddie poured Raven a cup and asked, "So, how was your day?"

Raven blew air out of her lips.

"Mirror travel?" Maddie asked, puffing her cheeks as if pretending to be sick to her stomach.

Raven nodded. "And a mouse and some pigs were afraid of me."

"How extremely silly of them."

"I thought so, too."

"No gloomy glooms. Let's see, what would cheer

you up?" Maddie scrunched her nose thoughtfully. "I know, let's play If I Didn't."

"Hexcellent," said Raven. She loved Wonderland games. "I'll start. Um, if I didn't sleep in a bed…"

Maddie shut her eyes tight, then opened them wide. "Then I'd nap in nice, warm bread!"

"Ooh, nailed it."

"I have a good one for you." Maddie smiled, and her blue-green eyes sparkled. "If I didn't have to be the Evil Queen…"

Raven felt her mouth open but had no words to speak. What would she be? It was a pointless question because she didn't have any choice in the matter.

"I don't know…." she whispered, feeling hollow.

"Silly, that doesn't rhyme," said Maddie. "I win!"

Raven felt stunned. Not from losing the game, of course. No one could beat Maddie at a Wonderland game. But Raven had never allowed that question to enter her before: *If I didn't have to be the Evil Queen…*

Maddie poured Raven another big cup of rose hip tea and plopped in three sugar pebbles.

"A tea party makes everything better," Maddie said.

Raven drank her tea and had to agree. Nothing

could be truly horrible as long as she had a friend like Maddie.

That's what Raven thought, anyway. It wasn't the first time Raven would be wrong.

"Why would Raven be wrong?" asked Maddie.

"Huh? What do you mean?" said Raven.

"Well, I just heard a voice say that you thought nothing could be truly horrible but that you were wrong."

"Aah…" Raven looked Maddie over. "I forget that the wild magic of Wonderland madness has some side effects. Like hearing voices. Hey, how about we find Cedar and go together to the Charmitorium?"

"Tea-riffic! Shall we somersault or walk?"

CHAPTER 4

MADDIE'S CHAT
WITH THE VOICE
Narrator

AND SO OUR CHARACTERS' LEGACY YEAR at Ever After High began.

Wait, who are you, Voice?

Oh! You really can hear me?

Of course I can.

Well, I'm the Narrator.

Hi, Narrator. I'm Madeline Hatter, and I'm really

enjoying all your clever observations and helpful information.

Why, thank you! No one's ever noticed before.

I'm pretty good at noticing things. I'm also good at standing on my head, eating three things at once, talking without taking a breath for a long long long long long long long time, picking out a good watermelon, and thinking up riddles—though I can't always solve them, at least not my own. Other people's riddles are easier to solve, don't you agree?

I hadn't thought about it before, but I shall try to observe. That's what I do best. And I'd best get back to it.

Okay! I'll be listening!

CHAPTER 5

THAT DANGEROUS WORD "Choice"!

RAVEN TOOK HER TRAY TO THE LAST TABLE in the Castleteria, her back to one of the trees that grew from the floor to the skylights six stories up. A leaf drifted down, plopping onto the surface of Raven's soup. She stuck her spoon into the bowl to flick the leaf out, but her spoon clinked against something unexpectedly hard amid the stewed carrots and potatoes.

"Heads up. It's stone soup again," said Raven as Maddie and Cedar Wood set their trays down beside hers.

Cedar groaned and picked up her spoon with her bright blue fingers. While the rest of her was the fiery brown of the cedar wood she'd been carved from, her fingers were covered in blue paint up to her knuckles. You could tell a lot about Cedar's current art projects by the color of her fingers. She didn't mind getting messy. She just sanded the paint off.

Raven fished the stone out of her soup and dumped it on her napkin. Cedar did the same.

Raven heard a crunch.

"Maddie!" said Raven. "You're not supposed to *eat* the stone."

"Why not?" said Maddie. "It's delightfully crunchy."

"How do you even do that?" Raven asked. "I mean, it's a rock."

Maddie shrugged. "Sometimes things aren't impossible the first time I try, because I don't know they're impossible yet. I probably couldn't do it again, though."

"Chewing rocks is just creepy and weird," Cedar said. She blushed, her wooden cheeks a deep orange brown. "Sorry! I can't tell a lie! But I like you! A lot! Whew, I'm glad that's true."

Maddie smiled, her teeth stuck with stone dust. "A pod for peas wears hearts on a sleeve."

"Riddlish alert," said Cedar and Raven at once.

"Whoops!" said Maddie. "I meant to say I like you, too!"

As a first-year student, Raven had been alarmed by her new friend Maddie's habit of suddenly speaking nonsense. But she quickly got used to her random bursts of Riddlish, one of the native languages of Wonderland. It still sounded like nonsense to Raven, but Maddie swore it made sense.

There were shouts of surprise around the Castleteria. Raven looked up to see fairy-godmothers-in-training *poofing* in, handing out class schedules, and *poofing* away again, appearing and disappearing in clouds of pink smoke.

A fairy-godmother-in-training handed Cedar a paper just before she *poofed* away.

"Oh no," Cedar said quietly, reading her schedule. "This year I have…Woodshop. All those saws…" She shuddered.

Another fairy-godmother-in-training *poofed* amid pink smoke in front of Raven. She held out the class schedule with a smile. Then, seeming to recognize

Raven Queen, she shrieked and disappeared. With Raven's class schedule.

Raven groaned. "Is it getting worse?" she asked Cedar, because her friend would always tell her the truth. She had no choice. She had been cursed with absolute honesty from the moment the Blue-Haired Fairy's wand touched the wooden puppet Pinocchio had carved to be his daughter.

"Yeah, it is getting worse," Cedar said reluctantly. "I think people have always been a little cautious around you. I know I was last year. It was kind of overwhelming, leaving Dad and our warm, cozy carving shop, coming to this massive castle of a boarding school with hundreds of new faces, and then, on top of it all, realizing that I was rooming next door to the daughter of the Greatest Evil There Ever Was." Cedar smiled and nudged Raven with her elbow. "Fortunately, it didn't take me too long to realize how unbelievably awesome you are. But this year—maybe because Legacy Day's coming up? Everyone's seeing one another not just for who we are but who we'll become."

"That's what I was afraid of." Raven dropped her spoon, no longer hungry. All the *poofing* had stopped. Everyone was looking over their schedules. Maddie read hers aloud: "Chemythstry, Riddling, Storytelling 101 . . ."

"Hey, wait!" said Raven. "I didn't get my schedule!"

Cedar looked around, concerned. Each time she changed expressions, her wooden face made a hushed creak.

"You'll probably have to get it from your advisor," said Cedar. "Who is it again?"

Raven sighed. "Baba Yaga."

Cedar shivered. "Sorry, Raven."

"Oh well," said Raven. "That's what I get for being a dark sorceress."

Before going to see her advisor, Raven stopped in her dorm room to change out of her spiky-heeled sandals. A visit to Baba Yaga's office required running shoes.

Raven spent half an hour walking outside the castle before she found the round, thatch-roofed cottage lurking in a stone courtyard. She stopped cold.

It hadn't seen her yet. On her tiptoes, she crept forward. She held her breath. Her sneakers squeaked.

The cottage turned slightly. Its two front windows seemed to look at her. The curtains lowered and rose again, as if blinking.

Raven smiled, trying to look harmless.

The cottage rose up on chicken legs and ran.

"No!" Raven darted after the cottage, leaping over hay bales and dodging carts and carriages.

"Not the pig field...not the pig field..." Raven muttered.

The cottage darted into the pig field. This was going to get messy.

Raven chased, mud and muddy-looking stuff that smelled worse than mud coating her black sneakers. She *squelch-squelch*ed. The cottage veered to the left. Raven leaped, scrambling for a hold on the front steps. There were several jarring bounces, and then the caught cottage stopped, settling on the ground with a sigh.

Raven wiped the sweat off her forehead. She scrambled to her feet on the front step and knocked. From inside came the sound of an indignant sniff.

"I smell evil," Baba Yaga yelled through the door. "Come in, Raven Queen."

The door swung in as if the cottage had inhaled

it open. Raven stooped under the low threshold and entered.

The room was smoky, lit from firelight, candles, and a hole in the center of the roof. The front windows, apparently, were just for show. The walls dripped with drapes; tasseled carpets swayed from ceiling hooks. Cages dangled everywhere, housing birds and lizards and creatures Raven couldn't name.

Baba Yaga sat cross-legged on a stool that appeared to hover slightly above the floor. Her long gray hair was knotted with feathers, snarls, braids, and small bones. Her skirt, shirt, and vest were drab, but her hands, neck, and ears sparkled with enough jewelry to please a sultan.

"You have come seeking knowledge or wisdom?" she asked.

"Actually, just my class schedule."

When Raven told her advisor what had happened in the Castleteria, Baba Yaga cackled. Where her mother's cackle was a thing of frightening beauty, her advisor's cackle invoked only fright.

"Some fairy-godmother-in-training was good and terrified, was she? Realized she was facing the future

Evil Queen herself? Ha! Good work, Raven. If you scare them, you're doing it right."

Raven mumbled something.

"Eh? What was that? Speak up! Don't mumble like a caterpillar."

"I said, I don't *want* to scare them."

Baba Yaga picked up a blue spray bottle and squirted Raven in the face with water, making Raven blink. "This is how I train my cats not to jump up on my spell table. They learn after a while. Maybe you will, too."

Baba Yaga considered Raven, then sprayed her a couple more times for good measure.

"Blech! You got it up my nose!" said Raven.

"You are a dark sorceress. Don't be a wet cat." Baba Yaga snapped her fingers, lifted her hand, and pulled a sheet of paper as if out of the air above. She handed it to Raven.

Her class schedule! Raven read it over with increasing horror: General Villainy, Home Evil-nomics, Poison Fruit Theory, History of Evil Spells, Kingdom Mismanagement...

"This is a major fairy-fail," said Raven.

"It all looks appropriate to me," said the dark sorceress advisor.

"I was hoping for at least a Muse-ic Class. Don't I have any choice—"

Raven stopped. The cottage got quiet, as if it had stopped breathing. The very air seemed to vibrate with that word: *choice*.

Baba Yaga studied Raven thoughtfully with those cold gray eyes. Then she sprayed her advisee in the face.

"Ack, stop. I'm sorry," said Raven.

"You should be. *Choice* is a dangerous word. You cannot throw it around idly, not in Ever After. Why the sudden interest in choice?"

Raven was tempted to confide in Baba Yaga all her fears about Legacy Day, but she looked into that face, all the wrinkles pointing down with her frown, and was certain the old sorceress wouldn't understand. So Raven just shook her head.

"*Hmph*. Headmaster Grimm won't tolerate foolishness during your Legacy Year. Take the classes you're assigned, and be grateful I don't change you into a worm I feed to my newt." Baba Yaga sniffed. Grime lined her wrinkles. "You may choose *one* class, and in the future, be more cautious when talking about choice."

Raven smiled. "Muse-ic Class, please."

Baba Yaga wrote with her pointy gray fingernail on Raven's schedule and with a gust of wind opened the door and sent Raven and her schedule flying out.

Raven pursued her wind-chased schedule, grabbing it out of the air just before it flew over a wall. Through a window she could see Apple meeting with the advisor of the princesses, Wonderland's White Queen. They were sitting in a real room on real chairs, drinking hot cocoa and apparently having a perfectly pleasant time. There was no sign of a spray bottle.

Raven picked up a stick and scraped at the mud and other stuff on her shoes. She could try to clean it with magic, but the magic might backfire and take her shoes off with the dirt, and perhaps her toenails for good measure.

She was on her way to her dorm to change when she passed Milton Grimm. Ever After High's headmaster was tall, his dark gray hair and mustache beginning to streak with white. He wore a suit, a vest, a tie, and a heavy key ring at his belt that jangled when he walked.

"Raven Queen. Visiting your advisor, I presume?" He indicated the mud drying on Raven's shoes and smiled.

"Yeah, her cottage ran into a pig field."

"So you chased it down? That's the spirit!"

Raven shrugged.

"Ms. Queen, would you step into my office for a moment?"

She followed him in. The office was as large as a throne room, and his chair was the throne itself, sitting on a dais behind a heavy oaken desk. Between the bookshelves lining the high walls hung the heads of long-dead mystical creatures. In a place of honor in the room's center and locked inside a crystal box on a gilded pedestal waited the Storybook of Legends.

Raven shivered as she passed it. She sat on the smaller throne before his desk.

He glanced up as if making sure the door was shut before he spoke. "Did you have your yearly mirror chat with you-know-who?"

Raven nodded.

"And you told no one? It wouldn't be good for

morale. Everyone but you, me, your father, Gepetto, and Baba Yaga believes the Evil Queen is no more."

"I've kept the secret for years. You can trust me."

He tilted his head as if he wasn't so sure. "And you didn't touch the mirror?"

"Of course not."

"It was a lot of work catching her and locking her away. I don't fancy another go of it. Your mother is a fine example of what can go wrong when a character doesn't follow her prescribed script."

Raven didn't answer. She'd heard this speech before.

"Ah, your class schedule. May I?" He held out his hand, and she gave him the paper. "*Hmm*...it all looks hexcellent, except for this Muse-ic Class. That's really only for Happily-Ever-After princesses to help them develop their signature power ballads."

"But...but I love music, and Baba Yaga said I could choose—"

Headmaster Grimm raised an eyebrow at the word, and Raven wished she could take it back. She could almost feel Baba Yaga's cold water squirting up her nose.

"Ms. Queen, last year was your Freedom Year,

when you had the opportunity to 'choose' your own classes. Now it's time to grow up. In your Legacy Year, all students must focus on who they will become. You are destined to be the Evil Queen."

"Yeah, about that. My mom wasn't just Snow White's Evil Queen like my grandma was, and great-grandma, and great-great-grandma, and great-great-great—"

"No, as I said, she overreached."

"Yeah, after her part with Snow White, she went off script in a major way! So what's my destiny? To do just the regular Evil Queen shtick? Or am I going to become like my mother and elbow my way into Sleeping Beauty and invade Wonderland and try to rule all Happily Ever Afters? Do I *have* to become the Greatest Evil the World Has Ever Known?"

He straightened. "Are you doubting me? Do you dare question me? I am Milton Grimm!"

Raven shrank in her chair.

The headmaster took a deep breath and put his slight smile back on. "Your story—and your very life—is far too important to risk on wild speculation." He erased Muse-ic Class from her schedule with a flick of his fingertip and handed the paper back.

"You must try to play your part. We all must, or our very existence is in danger."

"Yeah..." Raven started folding her class schedule into the shape of a heart.

"Raven." Headmaster Grimm smiled, but the smile didn't seem to reach his eyes. "You have so much potential. Don't waste it. Embrace your destiny."

Raven nodded.

She left his office and continued down the hall, past the first-years' lockers, hopping over the occasional toadstool. They grew at the base of the tree pillars but sometimes spread out farther, sprouting up between the floor tiles. Raven didn't like how they squished underfoot.

She heard music and followed it to the Muse-ic Classroom. Sparrow Hood was using the empty room for his band's practice session. They weren't great, but hey, it *was* music. Sparrow, in a green felt cap just like the one his dad, Robin, had made famous, was rocking out as the lead. The Merry Men backed him up on guitars, bass, drums, and one enthusiastic cowbell.

The music faltered when they noticed Raven standing in the threshold.

Sparrow smacked his chest with his hand. "I've been shot through the heart, men! Never have I seen such smoldering beauty."

In a moment he was kneeling before her, holding both her hands. He smiled up at her with a roguish grin. Despite herself, Raven had to admit that he was cute. He leaned in with puckered lips to kiss her knuckles—

"What-ever-after," said Raven, pulling her hands away. "I know you're just trying to steal my rings, Sparrow."

"Only for the poor—like me." He cocked his hat to one side and winked before backflipping away from her to his microphone stand. He struck a pose with one fist on his hips, one foot propped up on the bass drum.

Raven sighed. Hanging out with Sparrow was not her ideal pastime. But his band was the best band at Ever After High. Well, okay, it was the *only* band at Ever After High.

"Hey, Merry Men," said Raven. The Merry Men waved. The one holding the cowbell waved with the instrument in hand, ringing away.

"Let me guess…you've come to apply to be a

groupie?" Sparrow said. "You're in luck! We're now accepting this year's applications."

"Actually, I was wondering if..." Raven kept her gaze on her muddy shoes. "You know, if you auditioned female vocalists for your group, to do backup or whatever..."

She dared to look up. Sparrow wore a frozen expression of surprise.

"What—you mean *you*?" he said. "Can you even sing?"

"Hex yeah. Give me a shot and I'll—"

Sparrow laughed. "No, thanks."

"You haven't even heard me," she said.

"I don't have to. You're not singing on my stage. Evil cramps our style."

"I'm *not evil*!"

Sparrow backed away with his arms crossed in front of him, faking fear. "There she goes, men! Look out or she'll turn you into toads!"

The Merry Men laughed.

"You're already *toads*, so it'd be a waste of magic," she said.

"Hey!" said Hopper Croakington, son of the Frog Prince, who happened to be passing by.

Raven rushed past him and ran. All she wanted to do was go hide in her room and tell Maddie everything. She burst open her dorm door.

"Welcome home, roomie!" said Apple.

Maddie's side of the room had been transformed: redwood furniture, canopy, gilded chairs and wardrobe. Raven backed out and checked the names on the door: RAVEN QUEEN & MADELINE HATTER. She was in the right room.

"What's—"

"We're roommates now!" Apple said cheerily, folding her satin monogrammed underwear and putting them into her dresser. "I asked Headmaster Grimm if we could share a room, since we share a story."

"Oh." A year in one room with Apple. Was there no escape from the looming specter of her legacy?

"And look, I decorated your side for you!"

Raven's ebony furniture all had evil-looking spikes now—her mirror, her headboard. Her chair had been transformed into a spiny throne.

"Now you'll feel right at home." Apple smiled, waiting to be thanked.

Raven turned and ran away.

CHAPTER 6

NEVER AFTER AGAIN!

RAVEN WAS AN ODD GIRL. APPLE HADN'T expected much for her efforts decorating Raven's room—perhaps just a shout of joy, a sincere tear, or a hug and a homemade thank-you card. But instead Raven had been quiet since Apple moved in. Surly, even. Well. Apple would not let it get her down. The students of Ever After High depended on her to be dependably cheery. Especially at a party.

She finished getting ready by pinning a casual-wear tiara into her golden tresses and headed up to the Royal Common Room.

It was always elegant—marble floors, carved columns, sort of a fun-sized ballroom. But tonight it was simply enchanting. Briar had borrowed gold wire from Professor Rumpelstiltskin and crisscrossed it like streamers above their heads, providing perches for hundreds of live birds. Enchanted ivy was slowly growing, climbing up a wooden trellis in the center of the room. Beneath the trellis, Melody Piper was deejaying at the turntables, mixing an N-Chant single with some Lil Swain.

"Apple! You are totally fairest." Briar Beauty flung her long brown hair over her shoulder and gave Apple cheek kisses. As always, Briar was dressed to party, tonight in a loose silk top, tight pink skirt, black nylons worked with an edgy briar pattern, and super-high heels. Briar had started the crownglasses trend that was taking over Ever After High, and other girls always took note of Briar's outfits to stay current in the latest styles.

Briar thrust a crystal cup with a silver spoon into Apple's hands. "Whipped air. Try it. Totally invisible and *totally* good."

Apple dipped the spoon into the empty cup and

touched it to her tongue. The nothingness tasted like chocolate-raspberry swirl.

"Mm, this is amazing. You are the queen of parties, Briar."

"Yeah, well, you never know when you're going to prick your finger on a spindle and sleep for a hundred years, so I've got to live it up while I can!"

Ashlynn Ella rushed through the doors.

"Welcome to my Book-to-School party!" said Briar.

"Am I late?" asked Ashlynn, looking down at her mint party dress as if expecting it to turn to rags. "Am I late? I hate being late."

"You're fine. You're on time—don't lose a glass slipper."

"Oh good," Ashlynn said, quickly cleaning dirt from under her fingernails. "I went into the forest to help a mother fox relocate her nest and completely lost track of time."

"No sweat, Ash. Hey, could you be a dear?" Briar pointed up at the hundreds of silent songbirds. "I thought they'd sound spellbinding on the bass line."

"I tried earlier," said Apple. "But when I sing to

them, they just get frantic and flap around trying to save me from something."

Ashlynn spoke to the birds. They tweeted questions at her in bird language, she answered in her own words, and soon the birds were chirping the bass line of Melody Piper's music. It's a universal truth that birds love princesses, but only Cinderella's daughter understood their language.

More students arrived, children of famous princes and princesses, huntsmen, wooden puppets, and witches. When their parents, the Class of Classics, had ruled Ever After High, they had kept the royals separate from the commoners. But things had gotten more lax in their children's generation. Even though she was the royalest of the royals, Apple approved of the elite mixing with the commoners. After all, Headmaster Grimm often said, "You are *all* destined for greatness. There is no such thing as short stories or tall tales."

This was Briar's party, but Apple and the other princesses stood beside her as the welcoming committee: Ashlynn Ella, Holly O'Hair, Duchess Swan, Darling Charming, and Lizzie Hearts. Ever After High had more princesses than a theme park.

Blondie Lockes, one of Apple's and Briar's best friends forever after, also joined them. She claimed that her mother, Goldilocks, was a queen somewhere. Apple wasn't so sure, but Blondie was a sweetheart regardless, and—oh, those golden curls!

"Apple!" said Blondie. "I love that skirt. Not too short, not too long. Just right."

"Thanks, Blondie. Your boots are—wait, is that bear fur?"

"*Faux* bear fur," said Blondie, stroking the cuffs of her boots.

"Here comes Madeline Hatter," Duchess whispered, "madder than a hatter."

"How can you say she's mad?" Ashlynn asked. "She's the happiest person I've ever met."

"Not angry-mad," said Duchess. "She's crazy-mad."

"Maddie!" Briar called out. "I'm so glad you could—whoa, what are you wearing?"

"A dress," Maddie said simply.

She was, in fact, wearing a dress. But the neck of the dress fit tight around her knees, and the wide, stiff tulle skirt shot up around her neck. She had put it on upside down.

"Exactly, I put it on upside down," said Maddie.

That's what I just said.

"I know, I was just repeating what you said because no one can hear you besides me," said Maddie.

"Who are you talking to?" Briar asked slowly.

"The Narrator. Anyway, it was an accident, the whole me-putting-on-my-dress-upside-down thingy, because one can't see when one is dressing in a cheese closet. Obviously. But it somehow fit just right!"

Blondie smiled.

"I don't know how, but it looks crazy-amazing upside down," said Briar. "Like, seriously, I'm thinking I have to try that."

"I'm pretty sure none of my dresses would fit me upside down," said Apple.

"*Hm*," said Maddie. "Maybe *you* need to be upside down and the dress should be right-side up."

"Okay," Apple said without blinking.

"I've never been in the Royal Common Room!" said Maddie, gazing at the cozy ballroom. "The Commoner Common Room looks like the inside of a shoemaker's shop."

"So, you hexted me that you were bringing a roasted pig for the refreshment table?" Briar said, looking at Maddie's empty hands. Well, her hands weren't exactly empty. She'd fitted her hands with her shoes (and her feet with her gloves), but they were empty of any food items.

"Silly, I never said *roasted*," said Maddie. She removed her shoes, took off her large, striped hat, and stuck in her hands up to the elbows, digging around. There was a grunt. It hadn't come from Maddie. "Aha!"

Out of the hat sprang a pig. It began snuffling the floor.

"He's a darling, isn't he? And probably housebroken, since he appears to be hat-broken. I'm going to call him Snoof Piddle-dee-do."

Snoof Piddle-dee-do went around sniffing people's shoes as if hunting for treats. When he smelled the girl in the corner wearing a red cloak and hood, the pig squealed in terror and bolted away. The red-hooded girl looked around with wide eyes, as if checking to see if anyone had noticed.

"You know, the first time I met Cerise Hood last year she was wearing her cloak and hood, and I assumed she was just cold," said Apple. "But I've *never* seen her take it off since."

"Yeah, what's her deal?" asked Duchess.

"Nobody knows," Maddie said mysteriously. "Well, I bet the Narrator knows."

Of course, but I'm not telling. At least not right now.

Maddie stuck out her bottom lip. "Spoilsport."

The door opened as if by wind, blowing out candles. In came Raven.

"Whoops, sorry," said Raven, trying to grab the door before it slammed into the wall. "That's new."

Melody Piper stopped the music with a scratch. The birds swallowed their song. The Common Room became uncommonly quiet. Some students rubbed their arms as if they felt a chill.

"Oh, calm down," said Apple. "It's just Raven."

"Yeah, come on! Party time!" said Briar.

Melody Piper started playing music again, but the birds didn't join in. Briar reached up and nudged a bird with her finger, trying to get it to sing. The bird clapped its beak shut and shook its head, keeping one round eye trained on Raven.

"Hey, maybe I should just go...." Raven started to turn.

"Nonsense!" said Apple, taking her by the arm

and pulling her farther into the room. "You are my roommate and my friend. You are most certainly welcome. Everyone, be nice!"

The mood seemed to relax. Apple nodded, satisfied. She believed there was almost nothing a few encouraging words and a warm smile couldn't fix. Even back in nursery-rhyme school, Apple had had to scold the other children for being a bit hard on the Evil Queen's daughter. But this year—their Legacy Year—things were becoming more intense. Despite her mother, Raven had always been a nice girl. Yes, she would grow up to poison and rampage and try to destroy all happiness, but that was no reason not to be civil. And it was Apple's job as president of the Royal Student Council to set an example of civility.

"You look bewitching tonight, Raven," said Apple.

"Really?" Raven whispered. "Then why is everyone looking at me like I'm some warty toad?"

"Hey!" said Hopper Croakington, who happened to be passing by.

"Sorry, Hopper," said Raven.

Apple took Raven by the arm and walked her to the refreshment table, where Duchess Swan was sampling a cup of whipped air. Duchess had expressed an interest in running for president, too. Apple was sure she could count on her to be an example-setter.

"Duchess, say hello to Raven," said Apple.

Duchess stared at Raven with dark, unblinking eyes. "Hello," she said flatly.

"Hey, Duchess," said Raven. Then to Apple, "I really don't need to stay. I'll just go say hi to Maddie and—"

"Nonsense," said Apple. "You have every right to be here."

Duchess smoothed her feathered skirt and looked down her thin nose at Raven. "I don't usually hang out with commoners."

"Not that such things matter, Duchess," said Apple, "but Raven *is* the daughter of a queen—"

"An *Evil* Queen." A playful light danced in Duchess's eyes. "Looking forward to that, are you, Raven? Pretending to be nice all the time must be exhausting. I'll bet you can't wait to sign that book and embrace your future already."

"Not really," said Raven.

Apple started to suspect chatting with Duchess wasn't helping matters. She took Raven's hand and tried to move her away, but the Common Room was crowded and she bumped into Lizzie Hearts.

"Excuse me," said Apple.

"Off with her head!" replied the Queen of Hearts's daughter. "Did that sound commanding enough? I've been practicing."

Her pet hedgehog leaped from her shoulder, curled up, and rolled into the crowd, and Lizzie chased after him, shouting, "Step not on my pet or I shall call an army down on your heads!"

"Now *there's* a future villain who doesn't pretend," said Duchess, nodding at Lizzie Hearts. "She's destined to be an Evil Queen, and she owns it. Why are you so afraid to own it, Raven?"

"Back off, Duchess," said Raven. "Your story doesn't end any better than mine."

The feathers on Duchess's cap bristled. "At least *I'm* not a villain," said the daughter of the Swan Queen.

"At least my greatest ambition isn't to fall in love with a prince, only to lose him at The End."

"Now, you two, this is a party," Apple said as sugary and warm as fresh cobbler. Neither of them looked at her.

"Oh, wait, maybe I'm totally wrong. Maybe you

actually believe you *are* nice." Duchess tilted her head, looking at Raven with an expression of mock concern. "You poor, sweet child. Did your daddy lie to you when you were just a wee little hatchling? Did he promise you that you had a 'good heart' and that if you wanted, you could grow up to be just as nice and stupid and boring as he is?"

Apple held her breath. Her face burned. Not at Duchess's rudeness—Apple knew that Duchess desperately wanted a Happily Ever After, and any reminder that she wasn't getting one always ruffled her feathers. No, the heat was coming from Raven's hand, which had suddenly become hot. Summer-pavement hot. Four-and-twenty-blackbirds-baked-in-a-pie hot.

"Raven…" Apple said, carefully letting go of Raven's hand.

But Raven was staring at Duchess, her hands curling into fists. Duchess took a step back, the feathers on her cap wilting. Her expression said she knew she'd gone too far.

"Don't," Raven breathed. "Ever," she whispered. "Talk," she muttered. "About," she said. "My father!" she shouted. "Ever! After! *Again!*"

Apple ducked, putting her arms over her head, just as a swoosh of hot energy exploded from Raven. Fortunately for the partygoers, the magic burst upward. Unfortunately for the birds, it hit them dead on. The gold wires hanging from the ceiling swung wildly, and the birds were no longer birds. Fat, shiny snakes now clung to the wires with clumsy tails. They began to hiss. In alarmed unison.

Someone screamed.

The snakes couldn't hold on and began dropping down. Some landed on the marble floor with wet slaps. But most landed on people's heads and shoulders. More people screamed. The birds-turned-snakes were by nature afraid of snakes. They began to writhe about frantically trying to get away from one another, knocking over lamps and statues, the ones on the tables upsetting candlesticks and cups of whipped air. Invisible food splattered everywhere. Snoof Piddle-dee-do let out terrified oinks and charged through the crowd, desperate for any exit.

"Quiet down, please," Apple said. She tried to hum a calming sort of tune. But no one could hear her over all that screaming.

"It's the Evil Queen!"

"She's turning everyone into snakes!"

"Run for your lives!"

Snakes and people alike were trying to flee, but it was Raven herself who was the first one out the door.

Apple stayed behind to console Briar and help clean up the party. Duchess even volunteered to turn into her swan form, fly to Baba Yaga's cottage, and ask the dark sorcery instructor to come change the snakes back to birds.

By the time Apple returned to her dorm, Raven was in bed, her pillow (with a goblin-face pillowcase) over her head. Apple had bought the goblin-face sheet set for Raven. She'd hoped having evil items in her room would make her feel more at home.

Apple put a hand on her back. "Raven—"

"Please leave me alone," Raven whispered.

"Everything will be okay," Apple said. "It really will."

High school could be challenging at times, but life would be as Happy-Ever-After as it was supposed to be. Apple believed that from the tip of her casual-wear tiara down to her white faux-leather booties. She just wished Raven could believe it, too.

CHAPTER 7

THE ~~LOOMING~~ Goodness THREAT OF LEGACY DAY

No magic, no magic, Raven reminded herself over and over as she rushed from her dorm room out of the castle. After last night's disaster at Briar's party, she'd skipped breakfast in order to lie low. But there would be no skipping the Legacy Day practice. And there was no way to be inconspicuous in a high-collared purple top and black netting skirt. Curses, but why didn't she own any plain, boring clothes?

On the east terrace of the castle, Headmaster Grimm was already standing atop the pedestal. The white stone monstrosity was two stories high with red stone stairs on both sides. Just the sight of it made Raven shiver.

Stop being such a nursery rhyme, Raven scolded herself. *You are the future Evil Queen, so get over it, already, and don't waste any more of your teenage years worrying about it.*

"And though Legacy Day is still a few weeks away, I want you well prepared," Milton Grimm was saying. "It is an Ever After High tradition during Orientation Week for our second-year students to climb these storied stairs, stand at this fabled podium, and practice declaring your destiny. On the actual Legacy Day, when you say your name, your magical key will appear. You will insert it into the Storybook of Legends and turn it thirty degrees clockwise. Then stand, shoulders back, and declare your destiny to the world. Though, of course, we won't practice with the actual Storybook of Legends. Today"—he slapped onto the podium a thick book—"we'll be using a book of entirely reasonable school rules."

Maddie showed no concern as she bounded up the stairs for her turn. "I'm Madeline Hatter, and I pledge to follow the destiny of dear old Dad...the

Mad Hatter of Wonderland!" She pulled a cup of hot tea from her Hat of Many Things. "Done! Teatime?"

Hunter Huntsman was next. He threw back his broad shoulders as he declared, "I pledge to follow my destiny as the next Huntsman and to save Snow White and Red Riding Hood."

In line beside Raven, Ashlynn Ella moaned sadly. Raven perked up. Could it be that there were others like her who were less than excited to sign? No, that was wishful thinking. After all, as the next Cinderella, Ashlynn was guaranteed a Happily Ever After.

"It is I, Prince Daring Charming, eldest son of King Charming!" The prince had a lean, athletic build and hair so blond it was almost white. He smiled, his white teeth twinkling, and Raven heard several girls sigh. "I pledge to be the heroic prince who saves the fair Snow White!"

Apple waved at Daring from the crowd. Daring winked.

Daring's lanky brother Dexter, just nine months younger, jogged up the stairs, stumbling on the top step.

"Don't worry, little brother," said Daring, grabbing

Dexter around the neck and rubbing his knuckles into his hair. "Learning to climb stairs is tough. You'll get the hang of it!"

"Hey!" Dexter said as if offended, though he was smiling.

He grabbed his older brother in turn, and, laughing, they each tried to pull the other to the ground. Raven suspected this good-natured wrestling match had gone on throughout the brothers' entire lives.

"Your Highnesses, please," said the headmaster.

Daring let go and leaped down the steps, taking three at a time. Dexter straightened his thick black glasses and tried to smooth his brown hair, but a stubborn front cowlick sent it sticking back up again.

"Hi," Dexter said at the podium, his dimples showing. "Um, I'm Dexter Charming.... Well, I should use my full name, right? *Ahem.* I am Dexterous Charming, another son of King Charming, and I pledge my destiny to be... well, to be one of those Prince Charmings who saves princesses.... But, Headmaster, can I ask a question? I've never been clear about which story is my destiny...."

"Gallant princes are needed in many stories," said the headmaster through a megaphone from below the pedestal. "On the actual Legacy Day, when you make your pledge, the Storybook of Legends will show you your destined story."

"On Legacy Day? Oh, okay. I've waited my whole life to know. I guess another few weeks isn't so bad."

Raven watched several more students practice their oaths and tried to psych herself up. But when it was her turn to stand at that tall podium, she froze.

It's just a rules book, she reminded herself. *This isn't real. Yet.*

But the looming threat of Legacy Day was becoming as real as fairies in the Enchanted Forest. Raven didn't *feel* evil. She imagined her mother standing in that same spot many years before. Had her mother always been evil? Or had signing the book turned her into the evil person Raven knew? When Raven signed, would she suddenly lose herself and transform into that vain, angry, power-mad sorceress who had raised her? Or worse, would she stay the same Raven as always, but the binding magic of the Storybook of Legends would force her to do and say hateful things?

Maddie waved at her. Raven couldn't imagine her mother being friends with someone like Maddie.

Once Raven signed, would her friendships change? Disappear?

The sky was as bright and blue as witch's candy, but Raven shivered.

"Ms. Queen," Headmaster Grimm prompted through his megaphone.

"Right. Sorry. I'm Raven Queen, and I pledge to follow my destiny as…as…" She looked over the crowd. Everyone was casual, chatting with one another or looking out at the view of the Enchanted Forest and the mountains beyond. Maddie was playing patty-cake with her pet dormouse, Earl Grey. Only one face was turned toward her. Dexter Charming. Behind his thick glasses, his eyes were friendly, and his smile seemed so genuine the kindness took her breath. He'd been brave enough to ask a question. Perhaps she could be, too.

"Headmaster Grimm?" she squeaked. "Um, I have a question."

"Yes?" Headmaster Grimm said, his eyes narrowing slightly.

"I was just wondering…I mean…what happens when I take the pledge? Do I change into the Evil Queen just like that?"

Headmaster Grimm's answer came with the glaring beep of the megaphone. "You are promising to carry out your part of the Snow White story."

"Yeah, I get that, but what if…" She thought of Maddie's game—*If I didn't have to be the Evil Queen*…"What if I don't want to?"

There was a general gasp. Headmaster Grimm put down the megaphone and walked slowly up the stairs. Raven's mouth was too dry to speak, and her feet felt as cold as mermaid flippers.

He stood before her, arms folded. "Ms. Queen, don't even joke about such matters. You know the pledge is the greatest protection I can give you. Every citizen of Ever After exists as part of a story. If we don't retell those stories, they vanish and we along with them. *Poof!*"

Raven nodded slowly.

He put one heavy hand on her shoulder. "All will be well in The End."

Raven tried to smile as if comforted, but she barely felt her face budge. Headmaster Grimm held out his hand, inviting her to finish her practice pledge. But Raven couldn't muster the will. She pretended not to notice and instead plodded back down the stairs. At the bottom, Baba Yaga blocked her path. The witch snapped, raised her hand, and pulled something blue out of the air above her head. It was the spray bottle.

Raven shut her eyes as Baba Yaga sprayed her in the face.

"Sorry," Raven said, sputtering.

"*Hmph*," said Baba Yaga.

The practice went on, and Raven hung back against the wall, hoping her purple-and-black outfit allowed her to blend in with the shadows. But someone found her.

"Hey," said Dexter. "That was cool, what you said up there."

"It was?" Raven asked, blinking as if she'd just been sprayed in the face again.

"Yeah. I mean, I know Headmaster Grimm knows best and this is important, but sometimes I feel like we're not supposed to even ask questions." He kept his eyes on his hands. Raven noticed they were callused from all that sword training and princess-saving practice. "It was cool, you know, that you did ask. I mean, that's what I thought, anyway."

"Thanks," said Raven. Besides Apple, who was

everyone's friend, none of the other royals had ever talked much to Raven. "It must be nice having some mystery with your story, you know, not growing up under the pressure of knowing exactly what you'll have to do."

"Nice? I'd say it's more, um, not nice?" He laughed at himself. "I'm slick with the words, obviously."

Raven laughed. "What part is not nice?"

"Well, how everyone else has been able to recite their story since they learned to talk, while I'm facing this huge unknown. There is a story planned for me, but I can't plan for *it*, you know?"

"I'd never thought about that before." Raven straightened. "Do you know what would be most hexcellent? If we could get a look at the Storybook of Legends before Legacy Day. You know, see our stories played out there on the page—really just understand what we're committing to before we have to sign, right?"

Dexter nodded emphatically, his eyes never leaving Raven's face.

"Well…we could sneak into Headmaster Grimm's office and take a peek."

"Yes! But…*ergh*, I can't. My dad…King Charming…

super-strict…no break of rules…" He mimed his finger cutting off his head.

Raven slumped.

"But, hey, you totally should, Raven. If you think you should."

"Yeah, I kind of do. Dexter, do you think you could help me out with a distraction of sorts?"

Dexter's eyes lit up. "I love helping you. I mean, girls. I mean, anyone. I mean, usually people ask my brother Daring for help with things. Are you sure you aren't confusing me with him?"

Raven glanced over at Daring, who was flexing for a group of girls.

"Uh, yeah, I'm sure. You're clever—"

"You think I'm clever?"

"And brave—"

"You think I'm brave?"

"Well, of course I do. I mean, you are." Why did he sound so unsure? He *was* a prince, and a Charming prince at that. "So, anyway, I was wondering, could you keep Headmaster Grimm busy after this? Say, take him out of the castle and—"

"Ooh, I know! I could show him the catapult I've been working on in the sword-training meadow. He loves flinging cabbages over the wall. It's basically his weakness."

Raven smiled at him crookedly. She'd spent a year at the same school as Dexter without having ever spoken with him. He'd always just seemed like a slightly younger, slightly darker version of his popular brother. But she was beginning to realize that Dexter wasn't much like Daring at all. And in a good way.

"Thanks," said Raven, and she hurried off into the school.

She crept up the spiral staircase, past the Hall of Armor, and to the headmaster's office. Her heart was beating like blackbird wings. She tried the door. Locked, just as she'd feared.

"Vhat do ve have here, my cousin Gus?" asked a high-pitched voice.

From an alcove opposite Grimm's office strode Helga Crumb. Her blond hair was in curly pigtails, her red lips puckered. She wore a green dress embroidered with white flowers, knee-high socks, and hiking boots. The daughter of Hansel was never seen without practical footwear. One never knew when one might get lost in a forest.

"I do not know, my cousin Helga. Vhat do ve have here?"

Beside Helga stepped Gus, son of Gretel, wearing green leather shorts with suspenders and, of course, hiking boots. Besides different clothes and shorter hair, he looked identical to Helga. Their voices even sounded identical, with heavy vowels and *w*'s changed to *v*'s, *th*'s to *d*'s. Raven was never sure if that was their natural accent or if they just liked the way it sounded.

"*Hm*, it appears ve have a leetle lost birdie schnooping around," said Helga.

"If ve report leetle birdies schnooping where dey do not belong, Headmaster Grimm gives us a lollipop, no?" said Gus.

"*Ja*, he does, Cousin Gus. A strawberry lollipop."

Gus and Helga began to smack their lips as if imagining sucking on a lollipop. A strawberry lollipop.

"Hey, I'm not doing anything, so don't go tattle, okay?" said Raven.

"*Hm*, and vhat vill de leetle birdie give us not to tell, I wonder, Cousin Helga?"

"*Ja*, I wonder, too, Cousin Gus. Vhat vill de birdie give us?"

They both held out a sticky hand, palm up.

Raven leaned forward slightly, her eyes narrowing. Gus and Helga leaned back slightly. Their eyes began to widen.

Raven lifted her hands as if she would cast a magic spell. Gus and Helga held their breath.

"Run," she whispered.

"*Aah!*" they said, running away.

Raven laughed.

"Ve are not afraid of de leetle birdie!" Helga called from down the hall. "Ve are destined to cook vitches like her! Maybe ve vill practice on de birdie first!"

But for now, they kept running.

Still, it was too risky to break into Grimm's office when those candy-mad identical cousins might come back at any moment. Raven would have to wait for the right time. And the right distraction.

She was determined to see her story before committing to it on Legacy Day. Maybe her own story wasn't *exactly* like her mother's. Maybe she could play out her part without being truly evil. That was what she hoped, anyway.

When Raven was young, her mother had filled the castle with her own servants and allies. The Good

King hadn't been comfortable rubbing elbows with fiery-eyed warriors and scrabbling goblin hordes, dripping slime and chittering about the hexcellent flavor of people meat. Eventually the king and queen split the castle down the middle—his side and her side. The king lived in the smaller portion with the servants, and Raven spent half of each week with him.

On her sixth birthday, Raven's father gave her a puppy with curly white hair. Raven named him Prince. The next day, when Raven returned to her mother's part of the castle, the queen scowled at the dog.

"A *puppy*? What was your father thinking? A dark sorceress can't be expected to take care of a puppy."

"I'll take care of him, Mother," young Raven promised.

"You? But surely you're like me—allergic to all things cute and fluffy. *Hm*, I know what we need to do. Come, let's make a puppy potion."

Raven skipped after her mother to the dungeon workshop, wondering what a puppy potion might do. Make a puppy bigger? Enchant a puppy to help him fly or speak?

After mixing, stirring, boiling, and muttering, the

vial of black potion was complete. The queen told Raven to tip it over the dog.

"Here you go, boy," Raven said, pouring without hesitation.

The instant the black liquid touched the puppy, the bouncy, wagging creature transformed into a bone rat. Bone rats were five times the size of normal rats, with spiky black fur and glowing red eyes, and lived on a diet of bones.

"There, isn't that better?" the queen said triumphantly. "Powerful dark sorceresses like us are so much more comfortable with a bone rat for a pet."

"But…" Raven said.

"Raven, don't sulk," said the queen, her hands on her hips. "I'm doing what's best for you. Don't you want to grow up to be powerful and command an army of dark creatures? Of course you do. A puppy is only fit for one of those simpering, ballad-screeching, weak princesses who always do *good* and sit around waiting for a prince."

But…but I liked the puppy, Raven thought. *And the bone rat scares me.*

But Raven did not dare speak up.

The bone rat ran from Raven toward the queen, its

claws clicking against the stone floor. It wrapped its long, hairless tail around the queen's ankle and made a horrible, raspy grunt.

"What should we name him?" the queen had asked. "How about Bubonick? Come on, Bubo!"

The queen had started up the stairs, Bubonick following. Raven had just stood there, staring after them, the empty vial still in her hand.

Her mother was always saying, "Someday you'll grow up to be just like me!" Watching her puppy change into a bone rat had been the first time that Raven had thought, *But I don't want to be like you, Mother.*

From that day on, Raven was absolutely certain about one thing: She didn't want to be evil.

CHAPTER 8

BEWARE THE GLARE
OF THAT FAIR HAIR

F OR THE FIRST DAMSEL-IN-DISTRESSING
class, Apple and the other princesses met in
the back meadow, where four-story practice towers
awaited. They were made of glass. Each had one
window at the top. And no door.

Apple thought their teacher, Madam Maid
Marian, looked impeccable in a baby-blue satin dress
with blue netting hanging from a tall cone hat. Not
just anyone could pull off a cone hat.

"Translocation app!" Madam Maid Marian said

cheerily, pointing her MirrorPhone at Apple with no warning and pushing a button.

Apple felt as if someone was shaking her by her bones, and then suddenly she was high inside a tower. She paced on the cold glass floor of the fourth and only story, wondering how she was going to get out. Translocation apps only sent people in one direction, and couldn't be reversed. She watched as other princesses began disappearing from the meadow and reappearing in the other high tower rooms.

"There are so many princesses this year!" Madam Maid Marian shouted into a megaphone from the ground below. "You'll need to double up."

There was a glittery flash, and Briar Beauty appeared beside Apple.

"Yay!" said Briar, giving Apple two cheek kisses. "Being imprisoned with you will be such a Ball."

"I'm so glad you're here, Briar. I have to talk to someone. I am fairy, fairy worried about Raven."

"No chitchat, princesses, if you please," Madam Maid Marian said through her megaphone. "Now, how does one keep from getting bored in a tower? Yes, Holly?"

"An active imagination is every princess's friend," long-haired Holly called back from her tower.

"Well done, Holly! A girl can keep happy for years on end, so long as she has her own imagination to entertain her. As *you*, especially, will find out."

Holly's smile stiffened. She was Rapunzel's daughter, fated for a lengthy tower stay. Apple was relieved not to have a tower in her story. There would be a glass coffin, of course, but at least she'd be unconscious for that part.

"Now, everyone, please take a few minutes using your imagination to entertain yourselves," Madam Maid Marian called out.

Briar and Apple sat cross-legged on the floor. They closed their eyes to appear to concentrate. There was nowhere to hide in a glass tower.

"What's up with Raven?" Briar whispered, barely moving her lips.

"This morning Headmaster Grimm called me to his office," Apple whispered back. "He was glad I'd asked to be Raven's roommate. After her strange behavior at the Legacy Day practice, he's afraid that she might be doubting her destiny, and he fears what she might do next."

"She couldn't do anything worse than what she *will* do when she becomes the Evil Queen."

"Well, she could not become the Evil Queen at all," Apple whispered.

Briar opened her eyes and gasped. "No! Has she flipped her crown?"

"Hocus focus, Briar!" Madam Maid Marian called out.

Briar shut her mouth and her eyes. After a moment she whispered to Apple, "That's impossible. Queenness and evilness are her destiny. I mean, she doesn't really have a choice in the matter."

"You're right. I just need to find out what she's thinking. She's not very talkative with me, but Headmaster Grimm said I might be her only hope."

Apple heard the unmistakable twang of an arrow hitting wood. She took a peek. Madam Maid Marian pulled an arrow out of a nearby fence post and unwrapped a parchment from its shaft. There was a loud beep as she turned the megaphone back on.

"I have received an arrow message from Dr. King Charming. His Heroics 101 class spent the morning tracking swamp trolls. Prince Hopper Croakington got nervous, changed into a toad, and was promptly taken by a swamp witch for some undoubtably evil spell. Dr. Charming's prince pupils will be spending the morning rescuing Hopper and won't make it back to assist us here. This is quite unconventional, but"—Madam Maid Marian smiled—"it would appear you must escape from the towers yourselves. Surprise me."

Ashlynn Ella didn't hesitate. She leaned out on her glass windowsill and made a musical screech: "*Weee-aaaaaaa! Weee-aaaaaa!*"

A large golden eagle flapped to her tower, seized her shoulders with its talons, and flew her to the ground. Ashlynn landed delicately on the grass. After a few more *Wee-aaaa*s, the eagle went back for Ashlynn's tower-mate, Darling Charming, the Charming family's only daughter.

At the same time, Duchess Swan *poofed* into swan form and flew herself out of her tower.

"Oh, toadstools, now the bird thing has been way overdone," said Apple. She'd been about to whistle for a lift from her songbird friends, but she didn't want to be a copycat.

Holly was lowering Lizzie Hearts down from their tower with her own long hair.

"Can you go find a ladder for me?" Holly called down when Lizzie hit the grass.

"I shall return with an army!" Lizzie said, shaking her scepter in the air.

Apple was pretty certain Lizzie wouldn't be returning with an army, as the army of her mother, the Queen of Hearts, was trapped in Wonderland. A ladder would have been more helpful.

"Madam Maid Marian challenged us to surprise her," said Apple. "We need to do something unexpected...."

"I have an idea!" said Briar. "We could...we could..."

Briar's eyes rolled up, and she fell down, her head landing perfectly on her pillow purse. She began to snore sweetly.

Apple sighed. That girl slept more than Rip Van Winkle. How could she rescue herself *and* a sleeping Briar?

Apple began to pace, muttering to herself.

"Woodland creatures and gallant princes can*not* be my only options. Think like a queen, Apple. Solve this first and then solve whatever is Raven's problem. Headmaster Grimm says those who reject their stories cease to exist, and he's never wrong. Hocus *focus*, Apple! First you've got to get out of this tower!"

"Who are you talking to?" Briar asked, her eyelids half open.

"Myself. No one. I don't know! You fell asleep before telling me your non-bird-related escape idea."

"Falling asleep *was* my idea," Briar said, yawning discreetly behind the back of her hand. "Trying to eavesdrop."

Briar had lots of inconvenient naps, but the naps came with an advantage. While sleeping, she absorbed gossip spoken beyond the normal hearing range.

"Did you catch anything useful?" asked Apple.

"Madam Maid Marian whispered to Duchess that there's a secret way out of this candy jar."

Apple looked around. Glass roof. Glass walls. Glass floor. And nothing for four stories down. "What were Madam Maid Marian's words, exactly?"

Briar rubbed the sleep from her eyes. "She said, 'I wonder if someone will discover the secret escape. It was the architect's crowning achievement.'"

Apple got on her knees, running her fingers over the glass, investigating each crack, every divot. She discovered an imperfection in the glass that resembled a crown and pressed it with her thumb. With a loud, grating noise, a section of the wall began to separate from the tower. Its bottom slid farther out into the meadow, the whole section sloping down at an angle.

"Briar Beauty, you are brilliant!"

The girls squealed as they slid down the glass slide and into the grass.

"Well done, Your Highnesses," said Madam Maid Marian. "You are the mirror images of your talented mothers."

"Thank you," said Apple.

Mirror images... Apple was getting an idea of how to know what Raven was up to.

"Did you do the Princessology homework?" Briar asked as they walked back to the castle.

"No," said Apple.

Briar grabbed Apple by her shoulders and lightly shook her. "Who are you, you foul beast? And what have you done with my adorable friend? I demand answers!"

Apple laughed. "I was kidding! *Of course* I did my homework. I *am* Apple White."

Briar patted Apple's cheeks. "I take everything back. Except the adorable part. I thought I did the homework, too, but..." She pulled the assignment out of her backpack. The only marks on the paper were her name at the top and a dried pool of drool across the middle. It appeared she'd only managed to write her name before falling asleep on it.

"You can find the answers on page twenty-three of the Princessology hextbook."

"Thank you, Apple darling!" Briar shouted as she bounded off to the library. "I promise to name my first daughter after you!"

She was probably kidding, but Apple Beauty did have a lovely ring to it.

Apple had a few minutes before Princessology. The sooner she started on Project Raven the better. She needed to practice being the queen she would one day become. The Snow White story was like her kingdom. Would a queen sit back while her subjects rebelled and tore the kingdom apart? No! She would meet with the subjects, figure out what troubled them, and resolve their problems before any harm was done. So she would treat Raven like one of her subjects.

She'd already tried talking to Raven about the Legacy Day practice. But Raven avoided the topic like blind mice avoided a farmer's wife.

So…well…it might require just a wee bending

of the rules...but she was president of the Royal Student Council, after all...and solving Raven's problem was an urgent and vital mission. Since Raven wouldn't talk about it, Apple had to find out what she was up to another way.

By spying.

Now, how to get to the Mirror Lab without much fuss? She didn't have any practice in sneaking around. The moment she walked into the Great Hall of the castle, the whispering began.

"Look, it's Apple White."

"Isn't she beautiful?"

"She smiled at me. She really did. She smiled right at me."

How, exactly, did one go about trying to avoid notice? She thought of Cerise Hood and sort of folded inward, rounding her shoulders and looking down at her feet.

Immediately she was surrounded.

"What's the matter, Apple?"

"Are you sick? Are you hurt?"

"I'll save you!"

A flock of birds chirped and flapped around her head, and a friendly mouse squeaked at her toes.

"I'm fine, everyone, I'm fine! Thank you for your concern—truly."

Apple hurried away. It took several minutes, but she managed to lose her anxious groupies by hiding in a broom closet.

She creaked open the door, looked both ways, and ducked into the Mirror Lab. She was looking for an egghead to help her out. As luck would have it, Humphrey Dumpty was alone.

Humphrey's thin arms and legs sprouted from his smooth white eggshell body. He wore striped pants, a fetching tie, and round glasses. A prince among animate eggs, Humphrey always wore the famous crown that would break when he fell on his peaked head. All the King's Horses and All the King's Men hadn't been able to put his father, Humpty, back together again. Fortunately for Humpty, All the King's Women hadn't had much trouble. Apple hoped for Humphrey's sake that his The End would have the same luck as his father's.

"Hello, Humphrey," said Apple.

"Just a sec," said Humphrey. He was busy playing the video game *Call of Beauty* on the Mirror Network. He finished a level, paused the game, and looked up into Apple's clear blue eyes. He sprang to his tiny feet. The top of his head reached Apple's shoulder.

"Oh! Apple Wh-wh-white! Hi! Hey. I mean"—his voice lowered—"hey there."

"I need someone who is a wiz on the Mirror Network to help me out. And I thought, Humphrey Dumpty is exactly the prince who can save the day."

"Sh-sh-sure, Apple. Whatever you need." He put one foot up on the chair, fists on his round middle, taking up a heroic pose as if he couldn't help it in her presence.

Apple smiled. She could play the damsel-in-distress like a cow could jump over a moon. The male species couldn't resist wanting to help her.

"I need you to hack into the Mirror Network and track Raven Queen, giving me access on my Compact Mirror so I can keep an eye on her wherever she is. And I need this to stay between you and me. Okay?"

A moment of doubt seemed to cross Humphrey's eyes. Hacking into the Mirror Network was a big no-no. Apple needed to really sell this.

So she sang a little song. At the sound, a bird flew

in through the open window and landed on her finger. Apple accepted a gentle peck on her cheek, then let the bird fly away.

"Can you help me? Please?" she said, tilting her head.

Then she brought out her big weapon. She batted her eyelashes.

"Y-y-yes. Yes! Of course! Whatever you need, Apple."

Apple almost leaned in to kiss his smooth white forehead but decided that might be overkill. She didn't want him falling to pieces.

She felt guilty about spying on Raven, but the guilt passed as quickly as a butterfly. Looking out for Raven was in Raven's best interest. And in the best interest of their shared story.

Humphrey got to work, his little fingers tapping madly on his MirrorPad.

"Hey, Apple, do you want to hear the rap I made up about you?"

"Of course!" said Apple.

Humphrey turned his crown as if angling a cap to the back and began to rap while working.

Yo, yo, her name is Apple, and I can't grapple
with how fine and kind, you'd hafta be blind,
yo, blinded by the shine of her mind.
Gotta post a sign sayin'
beware the glare of that fair hair.
Can't bear the care of her stare.
One glance and you're tranced,
pierced by her lance, made to dance
to the boon of the tune of the
girl with the skin of pearl and golden curl.
She's Apple, yo,
and this be Humphrey on flow
with mo' rhymes I can throw
till the day she becomes Snow
till the Happily Ever then
till the chick 'comes a hen.
The.
End.

Apple applauded and smiled graciously. It was the least she could do.

CHAPTER 9

~~A HOT MESS OF WOLVES, SCREAMS, AND PASTRIES~~

A Basketball Game

WHENEVER RAVEN THOUGHT ABOUT Legacy Day, she felt sick to her stomach. Which was often lately, since Apple was bringing it up *constantly*. Raven couldn't put it off any longer. She had to look in the Storybook of Legends. Perhaps her story wouldn't be as bad as she feared. Perhaps she would see herself just pretending to be Snow White's Evil Queen, as if acting a part in a play, and then return to being Raven once Snow White married her prince.

But before she signed that book, she had to be sure.

Today was the day. Raven felt those bird wings of nervousness beating in her chest, but she wouldn't back down. She had spent days planning every detail.

She checked her bag for the fifth time, just to make sure she had enough wrapped caramels. She had to get through Grimmnastics class and double-check with Dexter, but as soon as the lunch bell rang, it was showtime.

"Why do you keep checking your bag?" asked Maddie as they walked to class. "Do you have squirrels in there or something?"

"Squirrels? Uh, no..."

"The squirrels in Wonderland always wore hats," Maddie said wistfully.

"You miss your home?" Raven asked.

"Oh yes," said Maddie. "Wonderland was wonder-landiful."

Raven's heart pinched. It was her mother's rampage that had forced Maddie and others to flee Wonderland, sealing the portal shut behind them—perhaps forever.

Maddie widened her near-constant smile and took Raven's hand. "But if I'd never left Wonderland, I wouldn't have met you!"

"Raven," said Cedar, "you have a smudge of ink under your nose that looks like snot—sorry! Sorry, I couldn't help saying it!"

"No, that's fine," said Raven, wiping the ink off. "I'd rather know than look like a fool."

Having an honest friend like Cedar was awesome. But she not only couldn't tell lies, she was also compelled to just burst out with the truth at random times. What if she knew Raven planned to sneak into the headmaster's office and was compelled to tell him about it?

No, Raven couldn't risk telling her. Or Maddie, either. Maddie meant no harm, but she just couldn't help talking.

Up ahead, Cerise was walking alone to class, draped as always in her red cloak and hood. Her broad shoulders pulled on the cloak, her legs muscular beneath her jeans. Raven wondered if Cerise was an athlete.

"From the first time I met Cerise last year, I assumed she'd become our friend, too," said Raven. "But I still don't feel like I know her at all."

"Listen to this," said Maddie. "Cerise Hood. Cedar Wood. Cerise Hood. Cedar Wood. Cedar, you and

Cerise *have* to be friends or your names will get mad and just march right off you!"

"What's she like?" Raven asked. Cedar and Cerise were roommates this year.

"She...she wears her cloak and hood to bed. She doesn't talk. But..." Cedar's voice dropped to a whisper. "But man, can she snore." Cedar smiled wistfully. "Do you think when I become a real girl I'll be able to snore, too?"

"Hey, Cerise," Raven called out.

Cerise looked at Raven and began to lift her hand as if she would wave back.

The Three Little Pigs came down the hall toward the Cooking room, and they bumped into Cerise. All three gave a high, piercing squeal and ran in terror. The first little piggy opened the classroom door. The second little piggy leaped through. The third little piggy slammed the door shut behind him. Raven heard the click of the lock.

Cerise pulled her cloak around herself tighter and hurried away.

"I wonder why she's so aloof," Raven said. "I mean, her story's a pretty good one. She's not even a villain."

The Three Little Pigs peeked out the window of the Cooking room's door, saw Raven pass by, squealed again, and dropped back down.

In the locker room, Raven, Maddie, and Cedar changed into their purple, red, and gold-striped Grimmnastics uniforms and entered the gym.

"The design is just so uninspired," Briar Beauty was saying to Apple, pinching the tank top and long shorts. "I could come up with a completely fabulous uniform. Picture this: pink leather, skinny silver belt, black knee-high boots—"

"Sounds lovely," said Duchess Swan. She didn't seem to walk so much as float across the floor. "But I don't think some students can wear anything as pale as pink, poor dears. The evil in them seeps out and stains the fabric." She looked at Raven and raised one thin eyebrow.

"Don't be such a toad, Duchess," said Raven.

"Hey!" said Hopper Croakington, who was standing nearby.

"Sorry, Hopper," said Raven.

Hopper shrugged. "It's okay. Toads are jerks. Now *frogs*, on the other hand—"

The tardy bell rang three times. The Grimmnasium

door slammed open, and Ashlynn Ella raced in, wearing a pale mint-and-coral dress.

"I made it on time! Did I make it on time?" With a poof and a sizzle, Ashlynn's dress dissolved into Cinderella rags. She hung her head. "I didn't make it on time."

Coach Gingerbreadman, wearing sweatpants and an Ever After High T-shirt over his hard cookie frame, came onto the court bouncing a ball.

"Welcome to your Legacy Year, kids. And Your Highnesses," he said, nodding toward the royals. "Let's start it off right. Everyone, grab a basket."

A few people groaned.

"That's right," he said, winking with one frosting eye. "We're playing basketball."

Everyone moved into their natural team structure: royals versus commoners. Though Raven was technically a royal (an *evil* royal), she felt more comfortable with the commoners, and no one argued. She draped a basket of treats on one arm and took the ball from their coach.

"And, go!" he said, blowing his whistle. "Run, run, as fast as you can!"

Raven dribbled, her team rushing down the court

toward where Apple's team was waiting, baskets swinging.

Raven passed the ball to Cerise, who was wearing her red cloak and hood over her Grimmnastics uniform. Cerise dribbled with one hand, holding her basket with the other. Daring Charming was facing her down.

"It's no use, Cerise Hood," said Daring. "I am a Charming—brave, cunning, athletic—"

Cerise faked left and dribbled right around him, driving toward the royals' end of the court.

It was then that Coach Gingerbreadman released the wolves.

While trying to dodge wolves, who were trying to eat the treats from their baskets, the students passed and dribbled, but mostly ran.

After Cerise made a shot, Daring got control of the ball, passing to Dexter over the heads of Raven and three wolves. The two brothers drove down the court, leaping over wolves and dodging opponents. Raven was so startled by Dexter's ability she just stood there watching. Who knew he was as good as his brother? Even Hunter and Cerise couldn't manage to get in front of them before Dexter made a slam dunk.

A wolf got Cedar's basket, so she was out. Blondie Lockes lost her basket, and Hopper Croakington lost his, making him so mad he turned into a frog on the spot. Kitty Cheshire disappeared and reappeared sitting on top of the commoners' basketball standard, kicking her legs and eating pastries from her basket.

"Kitty!" Coach Gingerbreadman shouted. "Get back on the court or you'll foul out of the game."

With her customary huge smile, Kitty faded away and reappeared back on the court, only to vanish again and reappear on the royals' basketball standard.

"You can't catch me, Coach Gingerbreadman," she said.

The coach sighed, and then quickly sidestepped a wolf who was out of bounds.

Cupid was flapping her wings furiously, rising above the court.

"Flying is against the rules, Cupid!" said the coach.

"But…but…wolves!" said Cupid.

Her basket slipped from her hands and fell directly into a wolf's open jaw.

Now that the wolves had had a taste of pastries, they were slathering into a frenzy, howling and yipping. Raven had no idea who had the ball. She held her basket above her head and concentrated on avoiding the snapping jaws of wolves hyped up on sugar. She almost missed playing simple, old dodgeball in nursery-rhyme school.

A salivating wolf was in hot pursuit of Lizzie Hearts, who kept shouting, "Off with its head! Off with its head!"

"I'll help you!" Hunter rushed toward Lizzie Hearts, pausing first to rip off his shirt, place his fists on his hips, and strike a bold pose. Out of nowhere, trumpets played a heroic fanfare.

"Oh!" Cupid said in surprise. The winged, pink-haired girl had transferred to the school just that year. "I didn't realize there would be so much trumpeting and tearing of shirts at Ever After High."

"Hunter does that," Raven whispered to Cupid. "The shirt thing. We're not really sure why."

"It's a Huntsman tradition," said Maddie. "I think they call it the Huntsman-To-the-Rescue Move. Keeps their shirts clean."

"Clean and ripped," said Raven.

"Well, write me into the list of Those Who Don't Mind a Bit," said Cupid, eyeing his perfectly toned arms and chest. "My, but he will break a few hearts."

"Hunter, Lizzie's not even on our team!" Raven shouted after him.

"Aw, he's a big sweetie pie," said Maddie. "A big, sugary banana slice of pie, cutie-sweetie Hunter."

A wolf ate Maddie's basket in one toothy bite. Maddie giggled.

Ashlynn was on her hands and knees, talking to a wolf. He howled back, nodding and rolling his eyes as if complaining about something in wolf language. She took a pastry from her basket and fed it to him on her palm.

"Someone throw the ball!" Coach Gingerbreadman called. But no one could find it.

"Maybe a wolf ate it?" Dexter offered helpfully. He was still running around, enjoying the game, though there wasn't much to call a game anymore. Just a hot mess of wolves, screams, and spilled pastries. Apple refused to give up, though, shouting out calls.

"Come on, team! No retreating! It's time to shine!"

Raven ran up beside Dexter, pretending to be on defense.

"Hey, Dex," Raven said. "Nice day for catapulting cabbages?"

He smiled, looked around to see if anyone was watching, then gave Raven the thumbs-up.

By the time the bell rang, the court was strewn with basket carcasses, pastry crumbs, and wolves with full bellies, beginning to snooze. Only one student still had an untouched basket over her arm. Cerise Hood.

"That's a win for the commoners!" said Coach Gingerbreadman.

"I insist upon a rematch!" said Daring Charming.

Cerise vaulted over a last hungry wolf on her way out. Given Cerise's story, Raven would have thought she would be afraid of wolves.

With a nod at Dexter, Raven left to change in the locker room. She slipped on her Coat of Infinite Darkness, once a gift from her mother. The long, black coat with dragon-scale details looked so good she almost wished people noticed her in it, but that would defeat the purpose. Even better was how it helped her blend with the shadows.

She stayed away from the bright windows in the faculty wing, watching till she saw Headmaster Grimm leave his office.

Gus and Helga were sitting on the floor in the

alcove, eating their lunch. Gus had a bag of bread crumbs he was stuffing into his mouth by the handful.

In her Coat of Infinite Darkness, Raven slipped by. Starting at the headmaster's door, she lay down a candy trail, looping down the hall and ending at Coach Gingerbreadman's gingerbread office.

She hid around the corner and waited.

"Vhat is dis, my cousin Helga?"

"I do not know. Vhat is dis, my cousin Gus?"

"Dis is caramels, my cousin Helga. Fat, juicy caramels."

"Someone has lost their caramels. Perhaps ve should keep them safe—in our bellies!"

There was the sound of crinkling caramel wrappers, followed by much munching and sucking.

Raven waited till the sounds faded down the hallway before sending Maddie a hext on her MirrorPhone.

RAVEN: R u in the Castleteria? Can you tell Blondie there's free porridge in the faculty wing?

MADDIE: Absotively. (:-)

Maddie ended all her hext messages with the emoticon of a smiley face wearing a hat.

Raven took off her coat and paced. In a few moments, Blondie Lockes came running up the stairs, her perfect golden ringlets bouncing.

"Raven! I heard something about porridge?"

"Porridge?" Raven said, playing ignorant. "I'm not sure. I was just standing here waiting for Headmaster Grimm to come back. But I did think I smelled something porridgey and sweet from the other side of his door...."

Blondie's eyes widened, and she sniffed the air like a hound on the hunt. She couldn't seem to help herself as she walked over to the headmaster's door and gave the doorknob a twist. The door opened under her hand, as one day the Three Bears' door would. Blondie had an uncanny ability to open any lock.

Raven followed her in, Blondie taking deep breaths through her nose.

"That's funny, I could've sworn..." Raven wandered over to the crystal case holding the Storybook of Legends. "I keep smelling something right here."

"In here?" Blondie put her hand on the case, and

the lock dropped away. "There's nothing in here but an old book."

Raven looked at her MirrorPhone. "Oh, wait, just got a hext that they're serving sweet porridge in the Castleteria. Sorry, must've smelled it through the vents or something."

Blondie swung her head around, like a predator listening for prey, and took off.

Raven shut the door quietly behind her. She had asked a goblin who worked in the kitchen to make a big pot of porridge for lunch, so at least Blondie wouldn't be disappointed.

Raven took a deep breath and stood before the Storybook of Legends.

The tome was covered in dark, cracked leather and edged with gold filigree. The Ever After High crest adorned the center. And as Raven suspected, it was locked. Asking Blondie to open that lock as well would have been too suspicious. Raven hoped something else would work.

She tried the pledge words she'd learned at Legacy Day practice to make her key appear. "I, Raven Queen, daughter of the Evil Queen, want to pledge my destiny."

No key. She'd suspected those words only worked on the actual Legacy Day, too.

So she tried all the magical passwords she could think of. "Abracadabra. Open sesame. Sim salabim. Alakazam. Hocus pocus. Voilà. *Please.*"

The book didn't budge. But then she had a thought. Headmaster Grimm loved that book. Raven would bet that he opened it regularly just to look through it. Maybe every day was Legacy Day to Milton Grimm.

"I, Milton Grimm," said Raven, "descendant of the Brothers Grimm, wish to open the Storybook of Legends."

A golden key appeared before her, hovering over the book. She plucked it from the air, pressed it into the keyhole, and turned it thirty degrees, just as the headmaster had taught.

The book opened. Magic crackled in the air with a smell like burnt nutmeg. The hair on Raven's arms stood up.

She flipped to the back and found her page. RAVEN QUEEN was spelled out in purple script. But for a short description of her destiny and a blank line at the bottom where she would sign, the page was empty. She tapped it, whispered at it, commanded it to show her story. But the page just sat there, page-like. She tried to view Dexter Charming's page, too, but no story-showy thing happened. Apparently, that only worked on the actual Legacy Day, too.

Raven rubbed her eyes, wanting to cry. She'd daydreamed about seeing her story play out, with a wild hope that it wouldn't be so bad after all. But no such luck. She'd have to wait till Legacy Day now.

Not looking for anything in particular, Raven began thumbing back through the pages.

There was Witchy Brew's signature.

Raven had been in the crowd last Legacy Day, watching that year's Legacy students approach the book. She remembered Witchy's sad face as she signed. Witchy used to paint watercolors of frolicking unicorns and once had helped Raven open her locker when it was stuck. But Raven had watched Witchy commit to becoming a villain who lures children into her home and fattens them up to eat them.

What Raven would promise to become in just three short weeks was even worse than a child-eating witch.

She thumbed back farther. All the tales were known to her: There was the son of the Genie's signature, the Goose Girl's daughter, Rose Red's daughter. There was the Ugly Duckling's flipper print, a Puss-in-Boots inked paw, the tiny scrawl of the Thumbelina.

And much farther back, her own mother's. The thick, looping signature took up half the page and showed no hesitation. Could it be that her mother was happy to become the Evil Queen? Eager, even? Raven sighed at her own pathetic self.

In the oldest part of the book, Raven discovered a page that was hauntingly different.

NAME: BELLA SISTER

STORY: THE TWO SISTERS

DESTINY: THE CRUEL GIRL WHO TRIES TO DROWN
     HER SISTER AND SO IS CURSED WITH UGLINESS

SIGNATURE:

Blank. It was blank. Whoever this Bella Sister was, she hadn't signed the book. But... but everyone signed. Didn't they?

Had Bella refused? Rebelled? The possibility

tingled and sparked inside Raven as if she'd swallowed a firecracker. Raven had never heard of the tale of the Two Sisters, but clearly Bella Sister was destined to be a villain, just like Raven.

If I didn't have to be the Evil Queen...

Her heart pounded; her stomach felt full of fire moths. Maybe Raven could refuse, too. Maybe she could rebel. Maybe she wouldn't sign the book.

But what would happen then?

Apparently, when Bella Sister hadn't signed, her tale had disappeared from history, since Raven had never heard of it. But what about Bella herself? Had she disappeared? Died? Raven felt a warm, pressing purpose rise up inside her. She had to find out more about Bella Sister. She had to understand what the next chapter held for those who didn't sign.

Raven locked up and left.

As she crept down the hall, she heard shouting from the direction of Coach Gingerbreadman's gingerbread office.

"As a general rule, Mr. and Miss Crumb, if something has a door or a wall or windows, it's a *structure, not* a snack!"

CHAPTER 10

THE UNSIGNED PAGE

THERE WERE MIRRORS EVERYWHERE IN Ever After High. And whenever Raven passed by one, the visuals streamed directly to Apple's Compact Mirror. That Humphrey was a genius! And his rap was a little bit catchy.

"*Her name is Apple, and I can't grapple,*" Apple sang softly to herself as she watched Raven pass the mirror in the Hall of Armor and enter the faculty wing. For some reason she dropped candy on the floor, then went back to Grimm's office.

There was Blondie Lockes. She opened the office

door. Blondie left, but wait...Raven stayed. Raven Queen! Using Blondie to break into the headmaster's office! Apple felt her pale cheeks flush a flattering pink.

There were plenty of mirrors in Milton Grimm's office. Through them, Apple spied on Raven speaking to the Storybook of Legends and opening it with a key.

A high wall mirror in the office gave an excellent view of Raven staring at her own blank page, thumbing the line where her signature would soon go.

But what happened next set Apple pacing in her dorm room. Raven found an old page with no signature at all. She just stood there, examining the signature-less page as the minutes ticked by.

No, Apple thought. *Raven couldn't be considering that. Could she?*

No one could honestly consider doing that.

But then again, someone had. Right there, a signature-less page. A story completely abandoned.

Apple's pacing became frantic. She had to do something. She raced down to the faculty lunchroom.

Baba Yaga was there. Alone. Except for a troop of Shoemaker's Elves. As small as mice and dressed in tiny knit shirts, pants, and caps, they squeaked happily to one another and scurried around the counter making sandwiches. But Apple didn't really count them as company. Shoemaker's Elves were notoriously bad at conversation.

"Pardon me, Madam Baba Yaga, do you know if the headmaster is coming here for lunch?" Apple tried to smile, but it wrinkled her nose. A cockroach appeared to be making a leisurely journey through Baba Yaga's long gray hair.

"I believe he is, at the moment, catapulting cabbages over a wall. You could wait." Baba Yaga spoke the words like a challenge, one eyebrow raised.

Apple would take that challenge. She sat primly on a chair, her hands folded in her lap, her ankles crossed.

Baba Yaga stared at her. Apple stared at the clock. The *tick-tick-tick*s seemed to come minutes apart.

"You don't have black hair," Baba Yaga said suddenly.

Apple sighed. "No, I don't." The older generation just couldn't let the blond-hair thing go.

"Your mother had black hair. It was part of the story. Snow-white skin, ebony-black hair, bloodred lips."

"I guess when it's my story, that part will change, since I was born a blond."

Baba Yaga leaned forward and said, "I find you extremely disappointing."

Apple swallowed. She decided she preferred Baba Yaga's stares to Baba Yaga's conversation. Apple was glad this old witch wasn't her advisor. Poor Raven! Of course, everything wasn't roses and peaches for Apple, either. The advisor of the princesses, Wonderland's White Queen, insisted they address her as "Mrs. Her Majesty the White Queen" at all times and made them imagine six impossible things before every Crownculus class.

Headmaster Grimm entered the faculty lunchroom, and was it Apple's imagination, or did the lights grow brighter?

"Apple White! How lovely to see you, Your Highness. Would you care for a sandwich?" A dozen Shoemaker's Elves lifted a plate above their heads, offering it to Apple. Between two slices of bread, she could see a whole fish, pickles, and a thick layer of grape jelly.

"I...uh..."

"Just ate, perhaps? I understand." The headmaster

whispered, "The Shoemaker's Elves are better at making shoes than sandwiches."

Apple smiled kindly at the wee little creatures as they lifted a huge turkey leg on a crane made of chopsticks and lowered it onto peanut butter toast.

"Looks fine to me," said Baba Yaga, digging a spoon into a ham sandwich that was sopping with milk.

"Headmaster, I came because...well, I'm concerned about Raven Queen."

Baba Yaga looked up from her sandwich to glare again at Apple. A fat bead of milk dripped off a wart on her chin.

"I adore Raven!" Apple assured her. "She's my roommate, my story companion, and...and my friend!"

Baba Yaga just kept glaring.

"Headmaster, could we talk in private?"

"Certainly, Your Highness," he said. "Let's go to my office."

Apple blanched. What if Raven was still there? She hadn't planned on telling Headmaster Grimm about the breaking-and-entering part. She didn't want to get Raven so deeply in trouble she would be expelled from Ever After High! What would happen to their shared story then?

He put his key into the lock, turning it. Apple didn't hear a click. The door was already unlocked. Had he noticed? He opened the door.

Raven! No Raven. Raven was gone. Apple exhaled.

Headmaster Grimm gestured her to a plush student throne and sat in his own grand chair behind his desk.

"You were saying…"

Apple cleared her throat. "I have reason to believe that Raven…that she…that she's actually thinking about *not* signing the Storybook of Legends at all."

Headmaster Grimm's forehead creased as if he were in great pain. "I feared that might be the case. Oh, to have stewardship of the young and have to watch them make foolish, dangerous mistakes! It pains this old heart, my dear."

Apple nodded, her eyes tearing up in sympathy.

"Does she realize—does she truly understand—that if she does not sign, she will simply cease to exist?" asked Headmaster Grimm. "And your story, Apple White, your story, too, unravels without an Evil Queen. I wish I could simply force students to make wise choices, but that is impossible. I am shackled, I'm afraid, able to only offer counsel and guidance."

His voice sounded so heavy and full of pain. Apple's eye released one tender tear.

"I want you to know, Headmaster, that I will do everything I can to keep Raven on the right path. Everything."

"That is a comfort," Headmaster Grimm said with a sad smile. "I'm glad you take this matter as seriously as I do. Raven *will* be brought to the light. How could she not, with a friend such as yourself? As you will one day be a noble and clever queen to your subjects, Apple White, I know you will be a noble and clever friend to Raven."

Apple beamed. He understood her! He'd noticed her tireless work in the Royal Student Council and the hours she spent checking in with even the smallest of students. Headmaster Grimm, at the least, saw the potential in her beyond just a pretty face. She would not let him down.

With a hearty farewell, Apple practically skipped out of his office and off to find Raven. She had a mission, and she embraced it completely. She had good reason to.

When Apple was six years old, she had fallen down a well.

She'd been chasing a dragonfly and climbed onto the well's edge. Then...a seemingly endless fall that ended in a freezing splash, struggle, and gasp for life. She treaded water, her heavy petticoats pulling her down. She didn't have the breath to either scream or sing for help. It was the first time in her life that she'd ever felt alone. Or cold. Or really, truly scared.

Every night before bed, her mother had told her a story that should have been frightening: *Scary Evil Queen. Huntsman ordered to cut out her heart. Lost in dark woods with grabby trees. Dwarves, dwarves, more dwarves. Old peddler lady giving her a strangling ribbon. Old peddler lady giving her a poisoned comb. Old peddler lady giving her a poisoned apple. Crunch. Gasp. Faint (beautifully). Dead sleep. Cold glass coffin. Empty dreams. Then...kiss. Wake. Prince! Cheering dwarves. Huge choreographed dance number. Happily Ever After.*

Even the scary parts of the Snow White story never scared Apple, because it was known. It was her mother's story, and her mother assured her that one day that same story would be hers.

Treading cold water in the well, feeling her legs tire, her face start to sink under, the cruel, smooth walls slick to her grasping fingers, six-year-old

Apple changed. She realized that the real world was much, much scarier than any fairytale. Only in her own story would she be safe.

It took two minutes for her servants, her parents, and a horde of woodland creatures to find her and pull her out of the well. Two very long minutes. By the time she was wrapped up in fifteen blankets before a fire, worried bunnies huddled on her lap, shoulders, and head, Apple had made an important decision. She wanted her story. She wanted it ASAP. The sooner she was in that nice, safe, familiar tale—poisoned fruit and all—the better.

Her story wouldn't happen without Raven. So Apple had to help Raven onto the right path.

And if that didn't work, she'd *make* her.

CHAPTER 11

~*A Villain ~~Hero~~ In Every Story~*

RAVEN WANDERED OUT ONTO THE EMPTY terrace, so full of thoughts she could barely stand straight. What had happened to Bella Sister? What would happen to Raven if she didn't sign?

She was about to sit in the shade of the massive pedestal and formulate a plan when she heard someone singing in a scratchy voice.

> *There you go again today*
> *Slaying dragons, vaulting walls,*
> *Battling goblin hordes alone.*

Raven peeked over the lip of the terrace. Dexter was on a lower balcony of the castle, cleaning bits of cabbage off his boots and singing to himself.

> *I would spin straw into gold*
> *Or sleep on a thousand peas*
> *To bring you safely back home.*

Raven grabbed some ivy and slid down to his balcony.

"Whoa!" Dexter said, jumping back. "Raven! It's you! And I was singing out loud, wasn't I? That's embarrassing."

"*It's enchanting to see you,*" Raven sang the chorus of the song, "*leaving in shiny armor, and it's enchanting to be me—*"

"You're a Tailor Quick fan?" he asked.

Raven shrugged. "I know it's not popular anymore to be a Quickian, but I can't help it. I usually go for music with a harder edge, but I just love her sound."

Dexter nodded, adjusting his glasses. "I think she just got too popular, you know? And then everyone wanted to be unique, so they refuse to like her anymore. But if a song rocks, then it rocks."

"Exactly. So you shouldn't be embarrassed, either."

Dexter laughed. "Yeah...but I'm a *guy*. My brother wouldn't be caught dead singing a love song. He wouldn't even be caught in a magical slumber singing a love song. But I..." He glanced at Raven as if wondering if she'd make fun of him. "I've always liked the idea of true love, like in the songs. Though I don't know if I'm destined for it."

"I wish I could tell you," she said. "The Storybook didn't show me my story or yours. I guess that only happens on Legacy Day."

She could see he was disappointed, but he tried to smile anyway. "Oh well. I mean, Legacy Day isn't so far away, right?"

"No, it's not." Her stomach felt cold.

He rubbed his hand over his head as if trying to smooth his hair flat, but it just stuck back up again. Raven liked it that way. Why did she suddenly want to confide in this boy? Having the Evil Queen as a mother was a constant lesson in not trusting anyone. But Dexter just seemed so...so *something*.

So she told him about the unsigned page. And he

listened, leaning toward her, his elbows resting on his knees.

"I want to find out what happened to Bella Sister all those years ago," said Raven. "But it's not like I can just look up in a phone book under 'Oldest Living Resident of Ever After' and find someone who remembers her."

"A phone book!" said Dexter. "Come on."

He grabbed her arm and pulled her, running inside and into the library.

The room was narrow but eight stories high, the far wall completely taken up by an enormous window. Sunlight filtered through the leaves of the library trees. Between the tree columns climbed seemingly endless bookshelves.

Dex sat at a mirror station and began tapping at the glass.

"I helped the librarians mirrorize the phone books during my programming class. I should be able to cross-reference the most recent phone book with the oldest and see if we can find any resident who was in both—aha! Look!"

On the mirror popped up one listing:

Old Man Winters
321 Cobblers Alley
Village of Book End

"Old Man Winters is, like, two hundred years old," said Dexter. "If anyone can remember, it'll be this guy."

Raven smiled at Dexter. "Check you out, totally rocking the prince-to-the-rescue gig."

"What? No, I mean, I just had an idea, is all. That's not really me...."

Raven knocked him lightly with her shoulder. "You're hard on yourself, aren't you? I get the feeling it isn't always easy to live with a perfect and popular brother. I think you need some better friends, Dex."

He looked at her, unblinking, considering. "If I do, will you be one?"

"You want to be my friend?" Raven said with a laugh. "That's not a frequent request I get from royals, especially not the closer we get to Legacy Day."

"Well, then let my request be the first," he said.

"I'd be *enchanted*," she said.

He laughed.

"But I don't want you to get too mixed up in my

evilness, Dex. I'm willing to get in trouble, but you don't need to."

His brow wrinkled. "I can see there's no point in trying to talk you out of it. Be careful?"

"Always."

Raven said good-bye and walked toward town feeling an unexpected lightness.

She hadn't even reached the Troll Bridge when that lightness evaporated.

"Raven Queen!" Apple was holding her skirt up to her knees to run faster. "Raven, I've been calling your name since the front doors of the school. Can't you hear me?"

"Sorry, I was lost in thought, I guess," said Raven, still walking.

"And I know what you were thinking about," said Apple, falling in beside her. "I know what you did in the headmaster's office. Raven, how could you?"

Raven stopped. "You know?"

Apple nodded.

"How?" Raven asked, squinting.

"I…uh…I was worried about you, and…"

"You were spying?"

Apple swallowed. "My dear, sweet friend—"

"You were *spying?*" Raven leaned back, shaking her head at the sky. "Is that why you wanted to be roommates, too? So you could tattle on me to the headmaster?"

"No! Please, Raven, I've been concerned—"

Raven turned her back and started to walk again. "Just go and tell him. He's determined to ruin my life anyway."

"How can you even joke?" said Apple, hurrying after her. "Headmaster Grimm is the reason the Land of Ever After is a place of peace and prosperity and perfectness! He is the kindest, the smartest, the best person. Why, if it wasn't for him, the Evil Queen—"

Apple stopped.

"No, go ahead, say it," said Raven. "The Evil Queen would still be rampaging, bringing ruin and evil rule to every kingdom in the land. I know what my mother is, Apple. And that's how I know I definitely don't want to be her."

"You won't. You couldn't. You just need to play the part you've been given, Raven."

"Easy for you to say," said Raven. "You don't have to be a villain."

"There has to be a villain in every story—an

antagonist, a big bad, someone to keep the heroine"—Apple splayed her hand on her chest—"from getting her Happily Ever After too quickly. I mean, without the antagonist, there would be no story! It'd be like: 'Once upon a time there was a girl who wanted to be loved, so she met a prince and got married and lived Happily Ever After, The End'? That's not a story; that's a bumper sticker."

Apple was walking with so much purpose now Raven had to jog to keep up.

"Don't you think you'd feel a little different about it if you were destined to be the villain?"

"No! I wouldn't! Well, maybe I would *feel* different, but I wouldn't act different. Every character matters. Can I help it if I was born to be the heroine? We all play the parts we're given—end of story."

If Apple was destined to be an evil witch, Raven *could* imagine her wearing warts and a pointy hat even to bed and practicing her evil cackle in the shower. Apple would commit completely to whatever part was hers. But Raven just couldn't—not yet.

They reached the bridge that led over the river separating the school grounds from the Village of Book End. They both stopped.

"Please understand," said Raven. "I need to know what happened to Bella Sister when she didn't sign. I can't sign until I'm absolutely sure it's the only reasonable choice, okay?"

"*Who dares to cross my bridge?*" came a throaty voice from down below.

"An innocent girl with no ill intent," Apple and Raven recited automatically.

"*Leave the toll and be quick!*" shouted the troll.

Apple and Raven had their coins ready and left them on the bridge post as they crossed. On the other side, Apple took Raven's hand.

"We share a story," she said. "If you change anything in your story, you change mine as well. Whatever you're doing, whatever you learn, I want to help. We'll do this together, okay?"

Raven rubbed her face and wished she could just zap Apple with some magic that would send her away and out of her hair. But what Apple asked was fair. Raven nodded.

"So…" Apple asked, fluffing her hair. "What adventure are we off to?"

"Finding Old Man Winters," said Raven. "He lives on Cobblers Alley."

The girls stepped onto the cobbled road. Dozens of small buildings nestled close together on Book End's Main Street, cozy as books on a shelf. Stores took up the ground floors, apartments in the upper stories. The warm, comforting smell of porridge blew out from the open door of the Three Bears Café, mixing with the chocolaty breeze from Hocus Latte Café. Mannequins in the front windows of the Gingerbread Boutique modeled the latest fashions. Raven could see Ashlynn Ella inside the Glass Slipper setting up a display of shoes, boots, slippers, and flip-flops. Raven was tempted to slow and window-shop, but she kept a quick pace toward Cobblers Alley.

The street there was barely wide enough for Apple and Raven to walk shoulder to shoulder, everything in shadow. Even in daytime, the street lanterns sputtered with light. Raven slowed to read mailboxes, scanning for the name Old Man Winters.

"I think that's him," Apple whispered.

Raven looked up. In an open space between buildings waited a drowsy green park. A white-haired man sat in a gazebo, stooped over to sprinkle crumbs for the pigeons. He wore a pale blue suit, roughened by time at the cuffs and hems. His skin was as pale as snow. His beard drooped from his chin and curled up like a cat at his feet.

"Excuse me, Old Man Winters?" Raven asked.

He looked up sharply. "Who is it? What do you want?" he asked. His voice was coarse and high.

"We're so sorry to disturb you, sir," said Apple. "Actually, you and I met once many years ago when you attended the Snow Ball at my home. I am Princess Apple White."

"Ah, yes, I remember," he said, relaxing slightly.

"And this is Rav—"

Raven shook her head slightly. She had a feeling this man might not want to help the Evil Queen.

"—my friend," said Apple. "We were wondering, do you remember—"

"I remember everybody and everything, and it's not easy, you know, keeping all that in this here noggin." He rapped his knuckles on his head.

"Yes, I can imagine," Apple said softly. "We heard of a lost tale about two sisters. Did you know them? Do you remember Bella Sister?"

Old Man Winters frowned and leaned back. "Now that's a name I haven't heard in a long time. Yes, I remember, and I'm the only one who will. When Bella didn't sign the Storybook of Legends, her story ceased, and she disappeared."

"Right then?" Raven asked. "The moment she didn't sign, she just *poofed*?"

"I don't know!" said the old man, straightening. "I wasn't there, was I? But she was never seen again. Neither she nor her sister. Cruel, if you ask me, condemning her sister along with her."

Apple looked at Raven as if asking whether that was enough.

"Do you know how we can learn more about her?" Raven asked.

"If you think I know everything, then you're wrong!" he snapped, his beard bouncing on his chin. "That is, I know more than anyone else, which is everything I know! But not everything that there is, is it?"

Raven looked at Apple. Apple smiled kindly at the man.

"Not everything, perhaps, but enough," Apple said. "If you have any idea of who we could ask for more information—"

"*Hmph*, maybe when she disappeared, she left her

things behind," he said. "Maybe you could find them somewhere in the school, and that will help. Now, that's all I've got to say. Look, your friend scared my pigeons away!"

The pigeons were huddled on the far side of the gazebo, shivering.

Apple and Raven left the narrow alley and walked down the bright main street. A sign in the window for Rapunzel's Tower Hair Salon advertised FREE MANI-CURSE OR PEDI-CURSE FOR NEW EVER AFTER HIGH STUDENTS!

"Thanks for helping," said Raven. "Old Man Winters didn't seem eager to talk to me."

"I am here to help you, Raven! And now we look for lost things. Where could we—"

"The Tea Shoppe!" said Raven, stopping in front of the building.

Apple tilted her head. "You think Bella Sister's long-lost possessions are in the Mad Hatter of Wonderland's Hat and Tea Shoppe?"

"No, but Maddie is. Come on!"

Raven opened the painted wood door, and the bell rang. The shop's walls were crowded with hats on hooks and brightly painted doors of different shapes and sizes. Even the ceiling had hats and doors. The doorless/hatless floor was packed instead with tea tables, every seat taken. It was always teatime at the Mad Hatter's.

"Where's Maddie?" Apple asked.

Raven was staring up. There sat Maddie, cross-legged on the wall.

"Um, what are you doing up there?" Raven called.

"Hi, Raven!" Maddie waved. "Well, we ran out of chairs, so..."

"But *how* are you sitting on the wall?"

"I don't really know, and I'm not sure I could do it again, but isn't it just so *much*?"

Maddie tried to take a sideways sip of tea, but the tea dribbled onto the floor. Her pet dormouse, Earl Grey, hopped off her shoulder, scurried down the wall, and lapped it up.

"Hey, Maddie, I could use some help."

"Ooh, I love helping!" Maddie put her hands in the air and slid down the wall, shouting "Wheee!" and landing on her feet. "What kind of help?"

"We're trying to find things an Ever After High student might have left behind a long time ago," said Apple.

"You're so good at finding things," said Raven. "Remember when you found my hat?"

"Yes, it was under your bed, right where it wanted to be."

"And my missing Evilnomics hextbook?"

Maddie looked at Apple. "Silly Raven didn't even think to look in her backpack…"

"And my backpack?" said Raven.

"…which had fallen out the window and was dangling from a gargoyle's nose."

"And my lost pen?"

"Yes, it was in my hair!"

"Yeah, I was never clear on how it got there… but if you were looking for left-behind things at the school, where would you start?"

"In my hair!" Maddie said brightly. She patted her hair all over. "Nothing except the usual," she said, holding up an ace of clubs, two tickets to the circus, a lollipop ring, and a hummingbird's nest.

"Where else would you look?" Raven asked.

Maddie suggested her hat, the sink, under a pillow, behind her back, in Apple's locker, under the front mat, inside a flowerpot… everywhere except the Lost and Crowned Office.

"What'd you say, Narrator?" Maddie asked.

I just made the point that you basically suggested everywhere *except* the Lost and Crowned Office.

Maddie wrinkled her nose. "The Lost and Crowned Office?"

"Wait, did you say the Lost and Crowned Office?" said Raven. "I didn't know the school even had one. That's a great idea! Thanks, Maddie!"

CHAPTER 12

MADDIE ~~BOTHERS~~ *Chats with* THE NARRATOR AGAIN

Hey, Narrator! Narrator, Narrator, Narrator, Narrator, Narrator, Narr—

I can hear you, Madeline Hatter. I can always hear you. You don't have to yell.

Oh, okay. Hey, good job back there! I never would have thought of the Lost and Crowned Office on my own.

What in Ever After are you suggesting? I didn't drop you a hint on purpose.

You didn't? Well, you were unpurposefully helpful anyway. Raven seemed really happy about it.

Hmph. I have to be more careful around you. It's my destiny to observe, not direct the story. Enough chitchat. I need to get back to it.

Can I listen?

Not unless you're in the next scene. Which you're not.

Oh, that's okay, 'cause it's teatime!

CHAPTER 13

DARKNESS
SCAMPERING

WHILE THEY WALKED BACK TO THE school, Apple worked on her MirrorPhone, downloading the Ever After High building specs.

"I've never heard of a Lost and Crowned Office," Apple said.

"I feel bad not telling Maddie about what I'm doing," said Raven. "She is my best friend forever after...."

Apple kept at her phone. "But she sometimes says random things and you're not sure if she'll out you at the wrong moment?"

Raven nodded. "My mother tried to take over Maddie's homeland." The Evil Queen, in her mad bid to rule everything, had poisoned the wild magic of Wonderland, polluting the land beyond repair. Maddie and a few others had managed to escape before getting infected, but Headmaster Grimm had had to seal the portal to Wonderland shut behind them. "If Maddie can be my friend, can look past who my mother is even after all she did to her home and her friends, then why can't everyone else?"

Apple thought, *You are supposed to be evil, Raven. It's not wrong for people to see in you your true nature.* But she didn't speak the words.

"Aha! I found it," she said. "The Lost and Crowned Office is on the dungeon level beneath the Charmitorium."

Raven attended General Villainy with Mr. Badwolf in the cauldron room, but Apple had never been down, down, down to the dungeon level. Just walking through that dank darkness made her feel as if spiders were skittering across her skin. The ceiling was low, and Apple felt they were always getting lower, pushing toward her head, trying to bury her.

At the end of a long hallway dug out of stone, they found a door. A small wooden sign read: LOST AND CROWNED OFFICE.

Apple opened the door. She was not surprised to hear it creak. They both pulled out their Mirror-Phones and turned on a candle app, bringing flickering light into the darkness.

Like a library, every wall was fitted with shelves, but instead of books, thousands of boxes filled up the walls. Overcrowded, piles of boxes had spilled onto the floor. And objects too big for boxes lay in heaps, covered in dust: giant teddy bears, a THIS WAY and THAT WAY signpost, several carousel horses, a particularly nice boulder, and a ghost.

The ghost was thin as candle smoke and all gray from her wishy hair to her washy skirt. She had a delicate little face with a tiny nose and pointy chin. She bore three smoky fingers on each hand, and they never stopped moving, stroking the air. Like a cat on the back of a sofa, she sat perched on the top of a large chair made of seashells.

"Boo," she said.

"Boo," Raven and Apple said in return. It was the proper thing to say when greeting a ghost.

"Are you lost?" Apple asked. "Can we help you find your story?"

"No, thanks," said the ghost. "I like it in here. So many treasures!" She flicked into the air and dived headfirst into a box.

"I've never met a ghost before," Apple whispered. "This is all very educational."

Apple tipped open the box lid, but the ghost was no longer inside. She shrugged and began to look over the boxes. Nothing was labeled. They would have to open each box and sort through the forgotten items, searching for anything bearing the name Bella Sister. Raven had climbed a ladder and was starting on the higher shelves.

"Why isn't this place called the Lost and *Found* Office?" asked Apple.

"Maybe if something's here, it isn't found yet? It's still lost." Raven rubbed her eyes. "There are a lot of boxes."

"Six hundred fifty-three thousand eight hundred and two," said the ghost, swimming in and out of boxes along a shelf, her ghostly skirt swishing like a mermaid tail.

"Whoa," said Raven.

"We'll never... That's... that's too many... I mean, I never give up on anything, but, Raven? Are you sure this is really so important?" Apple looked up from the second box she'd investigated. Only six hundred fifty-three thousand eight hundred to go.

Raven called to the ghost. "Have you ever noticed anything with the name Bella Sister?"

"Maybe..." The ghost poked just the top of her head out of a box so only her gray eyes were visible. "But I really can't let you find anything in here."

"Why not?"

"Well, then it wouldn't be the *Lost* and Crowned Office, would it?"

"I guess that's true," said Apple.

Raven went out the door, took down the sign, and brought it back in. She grabbed a marker from her backpack and added words:

LOST AND CROWNED OFFICE
and 1 thing found

"There," said Raven, showing her the sign.

The ghost stuck out her thin, smoky tongue. She

swam through a row and disappeared into a large box. It twitched and fell onto the floor with a thud.

Apple and Raven ran to it, their candlelight wobbling. There was no name on the outside, but when Apple lifted the lid, she found a notebook labeled BELLA SISTER.

"Thank you, ghost!" Raven said.

It was a large box, everything in it swimming in dust. Raven and Apple coughed as they brought out folded-up clothing, ancient shoes, and school hextbooks.

"This seems like a lot of stuff to leave behind," said Raven.

"It could easily be all her possessions," said Apple. "When she didn't sign, what do you think happened next?"

Apple held up a small, ragged doll. The kind a girl might have slept with since she was little. And loved so much she'd take it with her to boarding school. And never leave it behind. If she could help it.

Raven took the doll. "Maybe she…she had to leave in a hurry for some reason—"

"*Poof*," Apple whispered.

Raven opened the old notebook. The leather cover

was cracked, the paper yellowed. The pages were all empty except for a single drawing. It was a trollskin tree, the kind of tree that grows all in one night and then lives for hundreds of years, never getting any taller. Trollskin trees always had singular shapes—stout trunks with two expressive branches. In this drawing, there were black knotholes at the center, resembling two eyes and an open mouth. The artist had sketched an arrow pointing to the larger hole.

It seemed to be some kind of message, but Apple hoped Raven didn't think so. Apple was ready to put this little quest behind her.

"So that's that," said Apple. "Right, Raven? You have to sign the book or you go *poof* like Bella Sister."

Raven nodded. Apple wished she looked a little more sure.

CHAPTER 14

HER VERY NAME COULD
CAUSE AN EARTHQUAKE

SEVERAL DAYS LATER, APPLE STILL FELT covered in the dust and spidery feeling of the dungeon level. She hoped the field trip to the Enchanted Forest would breeze it all away.

As the troop of second-year students neared the forest, the blue-green smudge came into sharper focus as deep and colorful woods. Professor Poppa Bear, the Beast Training and Care teacher, led the way, with Headmaster Grimm beside him. The students followed them down the steep back steps of Ever After High, across the Saucy Stream on a wobbly footbridge, and into the clover meadow on the other side. Up ahead, the trees of the Enchanted Forest waited, all green and blue and golden. Bright spots of fairy light zigged and zagged through the trees, marking the trails of fairies like burning sparklers on a festival night.

Headmaster Grimm spoke as they walked through the meadow. "Playing your part in your story is so vital that all of nature will rise up to help you. Today an animal will be drawn to you, a companion of the woodlands, something that will aid you in your quest to fulfill your destiny."

"This is awesome," Briar whispered to Apple.

"All of us get pets today?" Ashlynn asked.

"Well…" Professor Poppa Bear arranged his spectacles on his furry snout and looked at his paws. He was extremely shy when addressing any girl. "Almost all. The Wonderlandians already had their pet companions when they came through the portal to Ever After."

Earl Grey squeaked something in Maddie's ear, and she giggled. Shuffle the hedgehog rolled around Lizzie Hearts's feet.

"What are you sorry lot of wolf dumps looking at?" demanded Carrolloo the caterpillar from Kitty Cheshire's shoulder.

"So, what happens?" Cedar Wood asked, still lingering back by the footbridge. "We...we walk into that forest and some creature comes out and grabs us?"

"No, silly. You do the Animal Call, of course!" said Maddie. "In Wonderland, all the children know the Animal Call. I'll teach you!"

Maddie began to chant while crawling, leaping, and hopping around like the animals she named.

> *Monkey, tiger, antelope*
> *Elephant, bunny, cantaloupe*
> *Mousey, guinea pig, skunky-poo*
> *Rat, turkey, chicken cordon bleu—*

"Chicken cordon bleu?" asked Apple.

"Sure, sometimes food can be a pet, too," said Maddie.

"Uh..." said Professor Poppa Bear.

Well, it was fairy, fairy strange, but magic often

was, and Apple was never one to shy from a challenge. The other students were surely looking to her to lead the way.

"Monkey, tiger, antelope," Apple began, taking the poses Maddie had demonstrated. The guinea pig pose got grass stains on her dress hem, and she wasn't really sure why chicken cordon bleu required her to roll across the ground.

"Er..." said Professor Poppa Bear.

"Tea-riffic! Now the big finish," said Maddie. She wiggled her bum while hopping and shouting, "Callooh callay, oh frabjous day!"

"Your Highness, there's no need," said Headmaster Grimm. "This Animal Call is unique to Wonderland alone."

"Callooh—" Apple paused mid–bum wiggle. "So...no?"

Headmaster Grimm shook his head.

Apple straightened out of the bum wiggle and smoothed her skirt. Her face burned, and she wondered if she looked more Apple Red than Apple White.

Professor Poppa Bear rubbed his snout and looked away politely. "For non-Wonderlandians, the animal call is quite simple. First you declare your name. Then you pull these spell poppers I have prepared for you."

He gave a bag to Hunter, who handed out the poppers inside. They looked like paper-wrapped candy in colorful foil, with ribbons on each end.

"I'm ready," Apple said, stepping quickly to the center of the meadow. Hopefully if she did the correct animal call immediately, the others would forget her bum-wiggle dance.

"I am ready as well," said Daring Charming, moving himself just one step ahead.

Apple smiled at him. Daring Charming was a hextbook prince: handsome, brave, clever, always ready with a sword or a winning smile. Apple was pleased with the mature way they handled their relationship. Yes, one day Daring would kiss her right out of a poisoned-apple death sleep and they would marry and have a beautiful baby girl (possibly blond, and that would be just fine). But their destiny was secure, so until then, there really was no reason to date exclusively.

"I am Apple White!" she said, pulling on the ends of her popper. With a *snap*, the foil ripped and a tiny ball of light shot up from the popper, rocketing high above the canopy of trees and then exploding into a white star. Daring declared his name and pulled his popper at the same time, his star blue.

At once, a white shape and a blue shape came rushing out of the forest shadows. The white shape leaped onto Apple's shoulder and twined around her neck. Ridiculously soft fur tickled her cheeks, and she laughed.

"A snow fox for Apple White," said Professor Poppa Bear. "And a peacock for Prince Daring."

"By the book, what a handsome creature!" Daring exclaimed as the peacock, tail fanned out, strutted around him.

Encouraged, other students began to shout their names, poppers snapping all over the meadow. Cedar remained by the footbridge.

"Professor Poppa Bear, I think I already have my pet," said Cedar, holding up her finger. A wooden cuckoo-without-a-clock sat there with wobbling eyes and bobbing neck. "If my pet, Clockwork, counts, maybe I don't have to—"

A woodpecker zipped out of the forest, looked Cedar in the eyes, and made a happy shrill sound.

"Aah!" Cedar ran away.

The overly friendly woodpecker followed.

"Aah, woodpecker! Help!" Cedar shouted. "Woodpecker! Girl made of wood! Not a good combo!"

"I'll help you!" Hunter cried.

"Here we go," Cupid said, rubbing her hands together. "It's shirt-ripping time."

Sure enough, Hunter ripped off his shirt and posed. Invisible horns played a heroic fanfare. Hunter lifted his ax and chased the woodpecker. Which was chasing Cedar.

"Aah, ax!" Cedar said, still running. "A woodpecker! *And* an ax! *Aah!*"

She ran faster. The woodpecker chased delightedly, with Hunter-and-ax in close pursuit.

Maddie jumped up and down. "This is so *fun*!"

"Should I try to zap it?" Raven called to Cedar.

But Cedar couldn't answer. She was too busy screaming.

"Oh dear, the woodpecker means no harm," Ashlynn said.

"Stop running, Cedar!" Professor Poppa Bear called. "The bird is just playing chase. If you stop—"

Suddenly Cerise's red cloak and hood streaked

across the meadow. She tackled Hunter, knocking him flat in the clover. Leaping from his shoulders into the air, she seized the woodpecker in her hands. She landed back on her feet in a dead run and, cupping the bird in her hands, carried it into the forest, where she let it go.

When Cerise emerged from the tree shadows, everyone was staring.

"Oh!" she said. "I just…I just wanted to help. Sorry."

Her lower lip quivered. She started to bolt again, but she must have squeezed the popper in her hand because a gray firework erupted above her head.

"Quick, Cerise, declare your name!" shouted Professor Poppa Bear.

"Uh…Cerise Hood," she said.

A gray fluffball bounded out of the shadows and began to rub his head against her ankle.

"Ah, a direwolf pup," said Professor Poppa Bear.

Headmaster Grimm scowled thoughtfully.

Cerise crouched down to pet the direwolf, and Apple saw her smile. Apple considered inviting Cerise to join the Student Council Activity Committee.

Perhaps some extracurriculars would draw the shy girl out of her hood.

"A baby bear!" said Blondie Lockes, rolling around in the grass, tickling her new pet. "I'm going to call him Grizz!"

Professor Poppa Bear sniffed. He didn't quite approve, it seemed, of the name or of a baby bear entrusted to Blondie—Apple wasn't sure which.

"*Yes!*" cheered Briar as a unicorn came bounding toward her. "I just knew I'd attract something fab-u-lous!" The unicorn lowered her head and let Briar pet her glittery mane.

Cupid was flapping her wings and doing happy spins in the air as a young Pegasus came flying toward her.

Hopper Croakington was staring at his pet, a luminescent dragonfly perched on his finger. Apple worried Hopper might accidentally eat it when in frog form until she saw the dragonfly breathe out a spurt of fire. It appeared the little guy could take care of himself.

Dexter Charming was sitting cross-legged in the clover, petting the jackalope on his lap. The furry bunny with antlers sniffled his nose, and Dexter smiled from ear to ear. Apple shook her head. Dexter was a nice kid but nowhere near the quality of his older brother.

Several more students still hadn't pulled their spell poppers. Apple couldn't imagine why on earth they were hesitating! The snow fox nuzzled her face against Apple's neck.

"All right, all students who haven't received their pets yet, follow me," said Headmaster Grimm. "No more delaying. Step into the forest and conduct the animal call."

Although Apple already had her pet, she felt it was her duty as president of the Royal Student Council to stay at the front of all activities. She fell in beside Raven.

"I'm calling her Gala," said Apple, as the snow fox ran in a circuit from her right hand up her arm, around her shoulders, and down to her left hand. "Isn't she perfect?"

"Uh-huh," said Raven, not looking. "Hey, check out that tree."

Apple sighed. How could any tree be more interesting than Gala, whose fur was as soft as the freshest snow? But then she noticed the trollskin tree right beside their path. Stout. Y-shaped branches. Markings that resembled two eyes and an open mouth.

"From the drawing!" said Apple.

"Shh!" Raven glared at her.

But the headmaster kept walking ahead of them, seeming not to have heard.

"Is that the same tree?" Apple whispered.

"Check out that knothole. Definitely large enough to stash something inside," Raven whispered.

Apple lifted Raven's hand, which still clutched the unpopped popper, and cleared her throat.

Raven frowned. "I had a pet once. A puppy. My mother turned it into a bone rat."

"What?" said Apple, horrified.

Raven shrugged. "She thought it was for the best, I guess, since I was supposed to be evil and all. But I've been a little shy of getting another pet ever since."

"Well, I'm sure this pet will be different. And even if it's a…a bone rat"—Apple shuddered—"we all get the best pet for our story. Aren't you curious?"

Raven looked at Gala and sighed. "Okay." She

pulled the popper. The firework burst green above her head. "I'm Raven Quee—"

The ground shook, as if her very name could cause an earthquake.

Thunderous footsteps. Crashing trees. A beast emerged through the brush. It lifted its green scaly head and puffed smoke through its nostrils.

"Dragon!" The scream came from a dozen mouths as the sound of fleeing teenagers filled the forest.

Apple picked up her long skirt and hightailed it like a deer for the meadow, Gala streaking white beside her. Only when she glanced back did she realize Raven hadn't run. She was just standing there on the path, staring up at the dragon.

"Daring!" Apple yelled to the prince, who was strutting with his peacock through the clover. "A dragon! And Raven—"

Prince Daring Charming pulled out his sword. "Say no more. You've bellowed your last furnace, scaly monster!"

He charged into the forest.

"Daring, stop!" said Raven.

But Daring didn't stop. He was running straight at the dragon, which didn't breathe fire. Or roar. Or swipe a clawed hand. It just sat there, staring at Raven, its dinner plate–sized eyes widening to platter-sized.

"Daring, maybe you shouldn't—" Apple started.

"Daring, I said stop!" Raven yelled.

"It's a dragon," said Daring. "I'm a prince. Slaying dragons is what I do."

He blew a kiss back at a cluster of girls, who giggled and waved. He sped up, raising his sword.

"Daring!" said Apple. "Raven! Don't—"

Raven yelled, "No!" She put out her hands and—

Crack. Poof.

Raven flew backward with the force of her spell, slamming into the dragon's belly.

And Daring was no longer running. In fact, he was moaning on the ground, covered in black sticky sludge.

The cluster of fawning girls sniffed and took a few steps away. Daring smelled like the wrong end of a pig.

"What have you done?" Daring cried from beneath the sludge. "I am dirty. I am felled. I am undone!"

"I'm sorry!" Raven said. The dragon was holding her in its huge clawed paws. "I just tried to cast a stopping spell, but it backfired. Naturally."

"Don't worry, Daring!" said Apple. "It looks like a Goo of Death Spell. I've read all about it, and it sounds worse than it is. I just need some hot water."

Apple whistled.

From the forest, birds and squirrels came flying with buckets of water and scrub brushes. Briar and Ashlynn offered to help, and without smudging their dresses, the three royal princesses washed away the sludge. Daring's fine white jacket was ruined, and his blond hair looked a little gray, but he was unharmed (except for his ego).

When Apple had rinsed off her hands in the stream, she went back into the forest.

Raven was sitting on the ground facing the dragon. The dragon lowered its head to her level, gazing right into her eyes. It snuffled, smelling Raven, her hair rising up on the gust of its breath.

"Not in the mood to spit fire?" she asked.

The dragon shrugged.

"Yeah, me neither."

Apple sat beside her. "That's no bone rat."

"Thanks for helping with Daring. I...I'm not good for anything."

Apple reached out and pet the dragon's tail. The

scales weren't slimy—just smooth and cool like glass. "Have you named her?"

"Nevermore," said Raven. "Isn't she a beauty? And a young thing, too, aren't you, girl? Only as big as ten horses, yes you are."

Nevermore scrunched up her face as if concentrating, and with a *poof!* she shrank to the size of a large dog. Now Nevermore could curl up in Raven's lap. Raven rubbed the dragon's belly, and Nevermore closed her eyes and hummed.

"Raven—" Apple started.

"I keep thinking, well, I just won't be mean," said Raven, as if they were in the middle of this conversation. "I may have to sign the Storybook of Legends and promise to be the Evil Queen, but I won't use magic or try to hurt or kill anyone and no one can make me, can they? But you saw what I did to Daring, and I haven't even signed yet. If I'm in the story, will I be able to help myself? I don't have a choice about who I will become. Maybe I won't have a choice about turning evil, either. Really evil. Want-you-dead-in-a-coffin-and-turn-puppies-into-bone-rats-and-poison-Maddie's-Wonderland-and-take-over-everything evil."

Apple sat beside her. Sometimes she couldn't think of anything comforting to say. It was a small weakness she was determined to mend.

Gala sniffed Raven's hand and didn't run away. Raven pet her head.

"I have to find Bella Sister's story, Apple," Raven whispered. "Before I sign, I just have to make sure there's no other option for me."

"Let's check the tree for clues," Apple said.

Raven nodded. "But not now. Too many people are watching."

CHAPTER 15

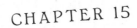 ~~Almost~~ Through the Wall of Briars

THE ENCHANTED FOREST HAD BECOME THE most popular hangout at Ever After High. All the second-years wanted to spend their lunch hours leaning back against the trees and playing with their new pets. Whenever Raven tried to sneak over to the openmouthed tree, Nevermore came running for her, snuffling. But Raven just couldn't get mad, 'cause Nevermore was such a cutie-sweetie dragon with those big red eyes and adorable spiky tail, aah…

But when Legacy Day was only two weeks away, Raven started getting a little more desperate. She persuaded Nevermore to go help Apple and Gala pick walnuts on the other side of the Enchanted Forest. Finally freed from her attention-grabbing pet, Raven sneaked up to the trollskin tree. She was just about to put her hand in the knothole—

"Well, hello there," said a deep voice.

Raven jumped back. It was Hunter with his pet griffin. Now it was Hunter's turn to jump back.

"Raven! Sorry, I…I was…not expecting…just practicing for a play…" He glanced around uneasily and rushed off, his griffin flying after him.

Raven sighed. It seemed even Hunter was afraid of Future Evilness Herself. She approached the tree again. She stepped on a twig, cracking it under her foot.

"Is that you, darling?" called a happy voice.

Raven jumped back. This time it was Ashlynn and her pet phoenix. Ashlynn jumped back, too.

"Raven! Sorry, I…was…talking to my phoenix, Sandella. Come, uh, darling!" Ashlynn said, her phoenix flying after her.

"I give up," Raven mumbled.

The Enchanted Forest was way too crowded these days. She decided to come back at night.

Raven waited till midnight, when Apple had been silent in her bed for some time, before slipping out from under her blanket. Yes, she'd sworn to include Apple in her quest, but the president of the Royal Student Council would *so* not approve of this plan.

Raven slipped on her Coat of Infinite Darkness and her most silent spiky sandals and opened the window. She grabbed hold of the ivy growing on the castle and shimmied all the way down to the ground.

She looked around to make sure she'd timed it right. No sign of All the King's Horses and All the King's Men. She'd been observing their security rounds for days, and they tended to go back to the barracks at this time each night for hot tea and scones.

Now for the thorny part.

Every night, one-hundred-foot briars grew up around the castle—a magical spell Grimm had designed for the students' protection.

Our protection, Raven thought grimly. *Or our cage.*

She walked around, peering into the thick, dark, spiky hedge, examining it for any holes.

"You can't just do stuff like this," said Apple.

"Whoa! What? Hey, *shh*," said Raven, putting her finger to her lips.

Apple stood there in her white satin nightgown, fluffy rose-colored robe, and bunny slippers, her fists on her hips. Raven's Coat of Infinite Darkness should have hidden her from anyone who didn't know she was already there. Apple was very smart.

"You can't just...just ignore rules and rush off to do crazy things. Rules are rules for a reason."

"My mom had rules for me," Raven whispered. "Rules like 'Always be evil; never be kind.' If she caught me being kind, I was punished. Dad had rules, too, and those ones I did try to follow. But how can I be sure Milton Grimm isn't more Mom than Dad?"

"Raven Queen! Milton Grimm is...is...why, he's *the* Milton Grimm! He's basically the mayor of the entire Land of Ever After. Even the kings and queens of the kingdoms bow to his wisdom. And you should, too."

"*Maybe,*" Raven whispered emphatically, trying to encourage Apple to lower her voice. "But before I turn my whole life over to evil and terror and despair, can I just be absolutely certain there's no other choice?"

"Yes, I suppose you should," she whispered back.

"All right, then. How am I going to get through this wall of briars?"

"How are *we*," Apple whispered. "We're in this together, remember?"

Raven sighed. "Yes, sorry. *We*."

Apple examined the hedge, tapping her finger against her chin.

"You could bat your eyelashes at it," Raven suggested.

Apple rolled her eyes.

A figure came tiptoeing through the dark. Raven and Apple froze. The figure saw them and froze. All three just stood there, frozen, wondering if they were seen.

"Ashlynn, is that you?" Apple finally whispered. "What are you doing out here? Leaving the castle at night is against the rules."

"I know. I'm sorry. I just…" Ashlynn tilted her head. "Wait, what are you doing here?"

Apple's mouth hung open. "Uh…official Royal Student Council business. Hey, maybe you could help us get through the briars? We just have some of that official business I mentioned. Outside the briars. At midnight."

Raven considered that Apple was as good at lying as Briar was at staying awake during Crownculus class.

"Of course. I'd be happy to help."

Ashlynn stood before the briar wall and smiled so sweetly, so purely, time seemed to go in slo-mo. She began to hum, a gentle lullaby kind of hum. The branches before her softened. They began to bend, then sway, like grass underwater. The swaying branches moved back, making a passage.

"Thanks," Apple whispered as she started through the opening.

Raven followed. Sometimes her roommate totally rocked.

Ashlynn kept singing. Her lullaby was so lovely, and Raven missed singing. Without even thinking about it, she found herself humming along on harmony.

Instantly the briar branches stiffened and whipped back into place.

Apple and Raven were caught in the center of the hedge.

"Raven!" Apple scolded.

"Oh, hex no. Sorry. Dark sorceress shutting up.

Ashlynn, can you try the humming thing again? I promise not to join in this time."

Ashlynn tried, but the briars wouldn't budge, too frightened of the evil sorceress in their midst, it seemed. And they seemed to be slowly growing, sticks and thorns pushing against them. A thorn bit at Raven's coat.

Not the coat, not the coat, she thought. A second thorn broke through the fabric. Raven glared, wishing so hard she could just cut loose and curse the whole big, stupid plant.

"I know who can help," Ashlynn whispered, and she ran off.

"Raven, can you use some magic and blast us out of here?" Apple asked.

"Oh, sure, yeah, I could try that. Hey, did I ever tell you about the time I tried to help a cat get down from a tree and instead of lowering the cat into my hands, the tree flung it high into the air? Yeah, imagine what I could do to you at close range."

"We need a prince," Apple said. "A prince will—ow! They're growing in!—A prince always saves the—ow!"

Just then, Prince Daring walked by as if out for an evening stroll.

Raven opened her mouth to call for him.

"Shh!" said Apple.

"I thought you said—" Raven whispered.

"I changed my mind," Apple whispered back. "Daring would *not* understand. Rules, you know."

"Then what's he doing out here breaking the curfew rule anyway?"

But Daring and his briar-chopping sword were gone.

Thorns were pressing against every part of Raven. One popped a button on her coat.

Another someone walked by. A prince? No, it was Hunter. And he had his ax. He always had his ax. He was looking around furtively, definitely not wanting to be seen. Too bad.

"Hunter!" Raven whisper-called.

Hunter jumped. He peered into the briars.

"Is that you?" he asked.

"Um, if you mean Raven and Apple, then yes," said Raven. "Can you do your choppy thing? Pronto? We're in a—ow!—a thicket, if you know what I mean."

"What in Ever After are you doing in there?" he asked.

"No time to explain," Apple said. "Would you be so kind?"

Apple smiled at Hunter. And then—yes—she batted her eyelashes.

He put a fist on his hip. "Of course! I—"

"But no shirt-ripping, if you please," Raven said. "Just the chopping."

Hunter was an excellent chopper. He didn't care that as he labored deeper into the hedge his own shirt tore and skin scratched. He chopped a tunnel straight toward and around the girls, clearing through to the other side.

The girls stepped free, shaking the severed twigs from their clothes and hair.

"Thanks, Hunter, really," said Raven. "Our secret, okay?"

"It was my pleasure to aid you." He looked between the odd pair as if very much wishing to know what they were up to, but he didn't ask and headed through the tunnel back to school grounds.

Just as Raven and Apple were running off, Ashlynn returned.

"There you are," she said to Hunter. As if she'd

been looking for him specifically. As if she'd been expecting him.

Could Hunter and Ashlynn...? No. It was a crazy thought. Ashlynn was destined for some prince, and Hunter was completely nutso for being the future Huntsman in Snow White's and Red Riding Hood's stories. Falling in love outside your story was completely forbidden, and Hunter and Ashlynn weren't the rebel types. Raven was just fooling herself, wishing that there were others like her who wanted a different destiny.

The moon was out, high and full as pumpkin pie. It seemed too bright to Raven as they crossed the footbridge. Hopefully All the King's Horses and All the King's Men were still on their scone break.

Apple and Raven ran through the meadow, eager for the shelter of the Enchanted Forest. Nevermore met them first. The dragon growled with joy, tucking her head under Raven and flinging Raven onto her back. Raven laughed between shushing noises.

"We're being sneaky, Nevermore, okay? Fairy, fairy quiet."

Gala was as silent as snow, silver in the moonlight,

and in moments curled around Apple's neck like a fluffy and fashionable scarf.

Nevermore carried Raven to the tree, only letting her off after Raven had given her underwings a good scratch and promised to come play the next day.

"Ready?" said Raven, suddenly feeling nervous.

Apple nodded.

Raven reached inside the knothole. It was deep. She had to put her arm in up to the elbow before she felt something. She pulled it out.

It was a piece of parchment, so old the edges crumbled with her touch. Holding her breath, Raven carefully unrolled it. The parchment began to crack. Apple read the writing aloud by moonlight as fast as she could.

Dear Brutta,
By the time you read this, you will know I ran
away. I am so sorry. I just cannot face Legacy Day.
I know that by not showing up to sign the Storybook
of Legends I will be condemning not just my story
to oblivion but yours as well. Will you forgive me?
As soon as I leave this note for you, I will go hide
from whatever magic the Storybook of Legends

possesses. Maybe if I am far away, it will not find
me and make me go poof. *If I survive, and if you*
can forgive me, please come find me. I will be
hiding in one of the Mystery Caves. You remember,
the one we picnicked in at the end of the yellow
sand trail?

I will wait till you come. I am so sorry. I hope I
am not making a terrible mistake.

Love always, your sister,

Bella

No sooner had Apple read Bella's name than the letter reduced to dust and was dashed apart by a breeze.

"It was still in the tree," said Raven. "I don't think her sister ever saw it."

Apple nodded sadly. "Because when Legacy Day came and Bella didn't sign, they both *poofed*."

"We don't know that! Maybe her sister just never checked the tree."

"Oh, come now, Raven. Headmaster Grimm says if someone doesn't sign, they and their story disappear, and here's evidence. So that's that."

"I guess we'll never know what really happened,"

Raven said with what she hoped sounded like resignation.

Apple raised one eyebrow. "You're thinking of going to the Mystery Caves to try to find the one she described, aren't you? The cave at the end of the yellow sand trail? And you're thinking of going without me?"

"No!" said Raven. "Well, maybe it crossed my mind."

Apple put her hands on her broad hips. "We're in this together."

"Okay, okay. Together. But how will we sneak away from school long enough to get to the caves?"

By the time they made it back through the meadow and over the footbridge, dawn was dawning. With the first peek of sunlight, the monstrous black briars around the school fizzled into shadows that wilted back into the ground. Apple followed Raven up the ivy and into their room.

They fell into their beds and had just closed their eyes when Apple's cuckoo alarm clock cheeped.

"Curses," Raven said.

"Rules...are rules for a reason," Apple moaned.

It was going to be a very long day.

CHAPTER 16

A MASSIVE ~~SNOOZE FEST~~ *Slumber Party*

OU'VE BEEN ACTING BRAINSWISHED lately," said Briar, trying on a pair of punch-pink heels at the Glass Slipper. "You okay?"

"Of course!" said Apple. "I've just been tired. I was helping Raven, and it's taken me a while to catch up on my sleep."

"Yeah, the last few days your MyChapter status has been 'drowsy.' I don't think I've ever been drowsy. I mean, I'm awake or I'm asleep. No in-between." Briar examined her brown hair in the mirror. "I was thinking of heading over to the Tower Salon and getting a pink streak put in. What do you think? Divacorn has them in her mane, and a girl's gotta complement her unicorn."

"That sounds spellbinding," said Apple.

"Hey, Briar. Hey, Apple," said Ashlynn, bringing in a stack of shoe boxes from the back room. She was the only royal with an after-school job. Her mother insisted she learn how to work hard. After all, she was going to have to spend a lot of her story mopping floors. "We got a shipment of fuzzy slippers just in time for the Beauty Sleep Festival."

Apple looked up from a pair of white platform sandals. "The Beauty Sleep Festival…"

All the royal tales got their own special festivals. In honor of the Sleeping Beauty tale, Ever After High held the yearly Beauty Sleep Festival. Everyone put on their pajamas and lay down on their beds, and a magical sleep spell rained over the castle, putting them into a restful slumber for two days.

Briar rolled her eyes. "I'd prefer my story got a dance festival with some kicky music and a chocolate fountain."

"It's kind of like a massive slumber party, so that's cool," said Ashlynn.

"Kinda," said Briar. "But the best part of a slumber party isn't the part where you're unconscious. I'm already facing a hundred years of sleep. Worst. Festival. Ever."

"You recall that the royal festival for the Cinderella story is basically just an excuse to get the students to clean the high school," said Ashlynn.

Briar laughed, putting her arm around Ashlynn. "That's true! But at least your Spring Cleaning Festival ends with a Ball."

Apple always enjoyed the Apple Festival in her story's honor—so many pies and turnovers and breads, and none of them poisoned. The whole school smelled of cinnamon and nutmeg for days. The Spring Cleaning Festival was an excellent opportunity to clean out her sock drawer and then wear a ball gown and dance till midnight. The Little Mermaid Festival took place every summer at Looking Glass Beach with swimming, beach volleyball, and a clam dig.

As president of the Royal Student Council, Apple had never missed a festival, even the comatose one. But it would provide two days when the entire school and faculty would be asleep and unaware if someone was gone. Raven was more important than any festival. Their *story* was more important.

Apple was looking over the display without really seeing, trailing her fingers over fluffy cotton squirrel and mouse slippers. "Briar, how far does the sleep spell reach? Into town?"

"Nope, it gets tangled in the Night Briars," she said.

Originally the Night Briars grew only during the Beauty Sleep Festival. But since the Evil Queen's rampage, Milton Grimm had increased security at Ever After High and now summoned the magical hedge nightly.

"All the King's Horses and All the King's Men ride beyond the briars before the sleep spell falls so they remain awake and kicking," said Briar.

"Of course, Headmaster Grimm wouldn't want dozing security...." Apple hopped in excitement. "I've been so distracted by classes and the Royal Student Council and Raven that I didn't even remember the Beauty Sleep Festival was tomorrow!"

"Well, if we have to sleep for two days, we might as well do it in style!" said Briar. "I need new pajamas that say I'm always ready to party. I am definitely not a flannel-nightgown Sleeping Beauty, if you know what I mean."

After shopping, Apple ran back to their dorm room. Raven was curled up in a chair by the fire studying her Home Evilnomics hextbook. Whenever she turned a page, the book made an evil cackle.

"Beauty Sleep Festival" was all Apple said. She was slightly out of breath from running, but she suspected the exercise had given her face a lovely sheen.

"It's tomorrow," said Raven.

Apple nodded, her smile excited.

"You mean…" Raven closed her hextbook. It cackled sadly. "We ditch it? Everyone will be asleep. No one would even know…."

Apple nodded again, still smiling.

"Apple, this isn't like you," said Raven. "To miss one of the royal festivals willingly?"

"I know you won't be satisfied until you've exhausted every possible lead. And I want you to be fully committed to our story."

Raven put out her hand. "Together," she said.

Apple took it. "Together. And now we've got to pack! What to wear? I think my red velvet travel cloak will look so elegant against the backdrop of a green forest. And—ooh—I love these white heeled sandals with the red apple buckle—"

"Apple," said Raven. "You realize we'll be walking. A lot. And it will be hard and possibly dangerous."

Apple stared at Raven for several seconds. "You're right. No heels."

She spent the entire afternoon packing and repacking. Birds and squirrels raced into her open window to help, but they weren't very good at making decisions.

"Does this skirt say, 'I may be hiking through goblin-infested mountains, but I'm still a pure, proper, intelligent maiden of royal birth'?" Apple would ask, and the squirrels would just tilt their heads and squeak.

Raven sat studying a map. "The water route would be the fastest, but the current flows the wrong way. We'll have to walk. The caves are a day to the east. That is, a day going over the mountain. Longer if we walk around it."

"Well, then," Apple said smartly, "we'll walk over it."

The only times Apple had been hiking, she'd been escorted by seven dwarf lackeys, twelve servants, eight armed guards, and a flock of seagulls carrying a net should perchance she slip.

There would be no safety net here.

But Apple refused to be afraid. Well, maybe she was just a little afraid. Still, once this journey was over, she was certain Raven would be convinced—and Apple's Happily Ever After secure.

CHAPTER 17

Biting ~~Cute~~ AND ~~Cuddly~~ Things
Slithering

THE MORNING OF THE BEAUTY SLEEP
Festival dawned as bright as leprechaun gold.
Apple and Raven ate breakfast with their own friends,
sneaking extra food into their bags.

By noon they were lying down in their beds, covers
to their necks, waiting for their check-in. Raven's
legs twitched. Her body did not want to be just lying
there. She was ready to run.

At last, a faculty member opened the door. It was
Professor Momma Bear, a sleeping cap pulled over
her furry head.

"Someone is sleeping in her bed," Momma Bear called out from the door.

"It's me," they called back in unison as they did each night at curfew check.

"Good girls. Nighty-night."

"Happy Beauty Sleep, Professor Momma Bear!" Apple said.

The moment the ursine professor closed the door, Apple and Raven leaped out of bed and grabbed their backpacks. It would be impossible to hide at high noon. Raven just hoped everyone was too busy settling into bed to look out the windows.

As they shimmied down the ivy, they could hear the Night Briars begin to grow, a whispery, clawing kind of sound.

"Hurry, hurry, hurry," Raven whispered.

She jumped down the last ten feet and ran, leaping over the low hedge. Apple was right behind her. Part of Raven hoped Apple wouldn't make it and then felt guilty for the thought. The briars were getting higher. Apple took a running leap, her shoes grazing the top of the growing hedge, the back of her skirt ripping.

"Should have worn pants," Apple said, breathing

heavily. "Note to self: Order custom riding breeches in white silk with red apple trim."

When they reached the bottom of the hill, Raven glanced back. The briars were a hundred feet high now. A pink cloud was gathering above the castle. It shook, and like a sifter sprinkling sugar on a cake, pink magic dust drifted from the cloud and powdered Ever After High. The billows of magic caught in the briars and spread no more.

Everyone inside would be asleep now. Raven envied them a bit. The Beauty Sleep Festival was a major power nap.

There was a whoosh of leathery wings and a streak of green. Raven felt a yank and suddenly she was high above the ground, Nevermore's clawed arms holding her tight.

"Aw, they must have sensed us leaving the castle," said Apple, sitting on the ground to pet Gala.

"Nevermore, sweetie," said Raven, "can you go small, please? We're trying not to attract notice."

Nevermore's huge nose wrinkled with a grimace. She sighed with a puff of smoke and shut her eyes tight.

"Wait—put me down before you—"

Poof. The enormous dragon was now the size of a large dog. And together, Nevermore and Raven fell. Nevermore beat her now smaller wings furiously, gripping Raven's arms. Their fall slowed, and Raven landed softly on a bush.

"Good girl," said Raven.

Nevermore spun in the air, pleased with herself.

They skirted the Village of Book End and headed out into the wide-open pastures. The day was sunny. Fluffy sheep bounded through the grass wearing bells around their necks and frilly bonnets on their heads. To the south, Jack's Great Beanstalk climbed into the clouds. They would have to steer to the right of the beanstalk farm, although that would lead them directly through the marsh—muddy, wet, full of biting and slithering things, not to mention a Marsh King who was known to pull the occasional girl down under the mud and make her his wife. Raven shivered, but the quest was more important than her fear.

With Nevermore by her side, the sun above, and adventure before her, Raven felt more hope than ever. Maybe Bella Sister had ended up all right. Maybe Grimm was mistaken about the fate of those who don't sign—or maybe he even lied. She usually avoided even thinking about the Snow White story, but suddenly it didn't hold as much fear for her. After all, she might actually escape that destiny! No spiky crowns and long capes, goblin minions and smoky potions, evil cackles in her throat, a crazy urge to kill Snow White, her fair stepdaughter—

Raven stopped dead in her tracks.

"So, wait, would I become your stepmom?"

"Huh?" asked Apple.

"In the story. Wasn't the Evil Queen Snow White's stepmom?"

"Well, she was in our parents' stories, but…" Apple stared, as if trying to fathom… but, no, it was unfathomable. She shook her head.

Raven scrunched up her face. "Just how would that work?"

"It will. Somehow. Each generation's story must be a little different than the last, right? I mean, I'll be a blond Snow White! You just have to trust that the story will work out in the end."

"Hey, I only *have* to do three things: Pay hexes, stay a queen, and die."

"What does that even mean?"

Raven shrugged. "I heard my mom say it once. As

you may imagine, she didn't like people telling her what to do and how to be."

"Yet she played her given part anyway."

"And then some." Wasn't acting out far more than her scripted part a rebellion against the Storybook, too?

The breeze shifted, and instead of the smell of sweet, sun-baked grass, Raven was slapped with dank, muddy air.

Gala and Nevermore stopped. They looked at the girls, their eyes sad.

"Oh, they can't come into the marsh," said Apple. "Maybe we're too far from the Enchanted Forest."

"Or maybe they're just too scared. They're still young. It's okay, girl," Raven said to Nevermore. "You can go home."

The small dragon flew up and snuffled her nose in Raven's hair, a kind of a farewell kiss. Gala streaked up Apple's leg and arm and ran circles around her neck three times before leaping off and following Nevermore.

When the girls entered the marsh, their travel slowed. The ground was as sticky as porridge, the gray mud slurping at their shoes. And the sounds!

Hissing, dripping, sluicing, slipping. Gucky, mucky, buzzing noises, and every one made Raven jump. Somewhere lurked the Marsh King.

"You know," Apple whispered, "if we'd already signed the Storybook of Legends, we'd be safe, and no Marsh King would be able to kidnap us, since that's not part of our story."

"Maybe," Raven whispered back. "If you believe what Headmaster Grimm says is true."

"Oh, Raven, sometimes you are so silly. Why wouldn't what he says be true?"

"Shh," said Raven. She'd heard a noise. A sloppy kind of footstep. Was it the Marsh King? If he so much as touched the sole of her boot, she would hit him with enough dark magic to fry his hair! So long as it didn't backfire on her. Which it undoubtably would.

She held her breath.

A frog jumped across the path, its wide feet slapping the mud.

Apple sighed. "Honestly, Raven, you get so worked up."

"Yeah, well, my mother sometimes read me stories at night. And you can imagine the kinds of stories she'd choose."

The Marsh King, the Boogeyman, the Scissorman, the Wendigo, hungry witches, angry tigers, and wicked sorcerers—these were the heroes of her mother's bedtime stories. And the subjects of Raven's nightmares. Young Raven had never wanted to root for her mother's heroes. She'd dreamed of reaching into the stories to save the poor girl sucked into the marsh or the little boy tricked into the witch's house. For as long as she could remember, she'd wanted to *change* the stories her mother told.

Raven had grown up with creatures of the shadows. Ogres? Excellent playmates. Goblins? She counted several as friends. But she never got over her fear of the characters from her mother's stories. Even now, if she woke up at night, she'd pull up her covers, afraid to look in her room and see the Boogeyman or the Scissorman. She still felt haunted by the monsters of her childhood.

Raven swatted the gnats in front of her face. Mosquitoes bit at her arms. She glanced over at Apple, whose blond hair was still perfectly curled, her outdoor-wear tiara tilted at a fashionable angle.

"Mm, I'd never been in a marsh before," said Apple. "It's so shimmery!"

Then the land just stopped. Water was everywhere. Not just the usual mud or dampness, but deep, scummy green water. Raven poked a stick in and couldn't touch the bottom. Only two narrow strips of semidry land continued forward, forking off from their current path.

They were so far into the marsh it would take longer to go back than go forward.

"In the story," Raven whispered, "there are two paths through the marsh. One ends suddenly, dumping the unlucky traveler into the water and the Marsh King's domain. The other leads to safety."

"Just . . . let's just avoid the water, okay?" said Apple. "I don't like swimming. Or rather, drowning."

"You should be able to float," said Raven. "Haven't you ever bobbed for apples?"

"Ha," said Apple.

They stood there, staring at the paths, wishing one looked—as Blondie would say—*just right*.

"Always take the right path," Apple said. "My mother taught me that."

So they went to the right.

Was this a trap? Was the Marsh King waiting at the end of the right path? Or the left? Or both? The buzz of mosquitoes sounded like scary music to Raven, warning the heroine not to go through that door! Don't go in the cellar! Run away!

And then the marsh ended. Woods waited, green ferns and grasses underfoot. Raven stumbled into the shade and sat, leaning against a tree, and took a deep breath.

"Raven, you were actually worried." Apple laughed. "You're the future Evil Queen! What Marsh King would dare mess with you?"

Raven laughed, too. "He wouldn't have known what hit him. Zap, pow!" she said, swishing her hands around. An accidental bolt of magic flew from her fingertips and hit a tree, wilting it instantly like a plucked weed.

"Whoops," said Raven.

"Please don't point your hands at me," Apple muttered.

They ate princess pea–butter sandwiches from their backpacks and continued on. At first the walk through the woods was pleasant. Raven found herself humming. There were no magic briars to get offended by the sound of the future Evil Queen's voice and snap around her.

She missed singing. Recently Headmaster Grimm had let her re-enroll in Muse-ic Class. She suspected he knew she was thinking of not signing and he wanted to win her over with kindness. But so far, Professor Pied Piper gave solos only to the princesses. Technically, Raven was a princess, but not the Happily-Ever-After kind, so, apparently, she didn't count.

And there was no solitude in boarding school. No private room with a private shower, where she could blast her vocals to the stone walls. Apple sometimes sang in their room, and though the sound brought birds to the window, it was hard to study to. Raven usually put on her headphones and tried to ignore her.

And she *never* sang in front of Apple.

But now, with just the woods and so many miles from the school, Raven let the hum turn into words, the words into a song.

> *Follow the river to the woods and take the path on the right.*
> *Take the right path that won't end in a bath, the path that leads through the night.*

"You have a nice voice," said Apple.

Raven stopped, embarrassed. "Thanks."

Apple started singing the tune. With Apple taking melody, Raven slipped lower into harmony. She had to admit, they sounded hexcellent together. Apple's high, pure soprano against Raven's soulful alto seemed the perfect mix. And they sang through brambles and ferns and bushes till they noticed their groupies. A flock of hummingbirds was buzzing madly around Apple's head, keeping a safe distance from the Evil Queen's daughter. A crew of bats with black leathery wings swooped after Raven.

At least the bats were eating the last of the gnats that had trailed her from the marsh.

Suddenly the hummingbirds were gone. Raven and Apple stopped singing. The woods were getting deeper. Darker. The hair on Raven's arms stood up. The air felt full of unseen lightning.

CHAPTER 18

PLUMP RED
APPLE ~~WHITE~~

NIGHT ONCE-UPONED ALL AROUND THEM, and still they walked. Apple thought longingly of riding in a nice, comfy Hybrid Carriage with quality shock absorbers. But even if they'd had a carriage, there was no road out here.

And no more squirrels. Apple found that alarming. What kind of woods was completely bereft of squirrels? She whistled a happy tune. No songbird whistled back. Woodland creatures knew not to come out here, it seemed. If it wasn't safe for them, was it safe for Apple?

She just had to get through this, Apple reminded herself. Once this quest was over, Raven would be convinced and sign the Storybook of Legends, and the rest of Apple's life would be safely nestled in the story she knew and loved.

She took comfort and tried to enjoy the scenery. The occasional trollskin tree seemed to look at them, the black spots on their bark like wide eyes, their two branches gesturing madly. Dark strips of moss hung from the trees and tickled them like spiderwebs. Apple thought she saw a bird at last up on a tree branch. She sang out to it. But the thing moved across the branch—not hopping but scurrying, its legs clicking against the bark. A very large spider? Or...something else?

"I've got mother-goosebumps," Apple whispered.

"It is pretty creepy here," said Raven.

Apple startled. "Is that wolf looking at us?"

"What wolf?"

"Right there!" said Apple, pointing.

"Um...you mean that tree stump? You're nearsighted, aren't you?"

"What? Don't be ridiculous."

"Apple, you squint at things all the time, and I've

seen your glasses case on your desk. You don't have to hide with me. I'm not going to think you're less-than-perfect if you wear glasses."

Apple sniffed. She pulled her red-framed glasses out of her backpack and slid them on.

Really, the view didn't improve any with clearer vision. The air was musty and thick, as if they were deep in a dungeon. A nice, friendly ghost would have improved this woods. Apple wondered if coming had been a mistake.

But—no. She straightened her shoulders and walked a little faster. She was here to convince Raven and save her story. At least it wasn't raining.

It started to rain.

Apple attached the rain visor to her outdoors-wear tiara and put on her raincoat—it was royal red, the same shade as her nail polish. Ahead, the trees cleared and rocks rose.

"This is where we save time by going over instead of around," Raven said, gripping a travel-size umbrella. "But it's not going to be pleasant."

Apple nodded. She stood tall and walked on.

An hour later they found themselves hiking up the wickedest fairytale cliffs ever known to story. The higher they climbed, the harder the wind blew. The rain slashed sideways, making it difficult to see, even with glasses.

The rocks were as sharp as daggers. One fall would chop Apple to pieces. She tried to sing, but if any helpful woodland creatures were nearby, the wind whipped her song away before they could hear.

Raven was shouting something, but the storm buried the sound.

"What?" Apple shouted back.

Raven pointed down. Apple couldn't see anything—the night was black, the storm was gray. Then lightning briefly lit the sky.

They were teetering on the edge of a cliff.

The way before them was craggy, high, and impossible to get over. The way they'd come was slick and sharp and impossible to get back down. And a dangerously steep cliff waited at their feet.

Apple sang desperately.

"There aren't any helpful woodland creatures out here!" said Raven. "But there might be..."

"What?" Apple shouted back.

"Well, creatures that would serve *me*," Raven said.

Apple frowned, not understanding.

"Help!" Raven shouted. "Help! I am Raven Queen, and I command someone to come to my aid!"

The mountain trembled, and the sound of grating rocks reached Apple's ears.

Apple could see torchlight on a ledge far down the cliff. She made a triumphant noise in her throat. Rescued! Would it be helpful woodsmen? A wandering prince and his hunting party? Or perhaps a fairy godmother disguised as an old witch? Apple couldn't see much besides the torchlight. Which kept multiplying. There must have been at least fifty people on that ledge now. She dried the raindrops off her glasses and put them back on to get a better look.

Goblins.

Goblins tall and short, wide and thin, all with skin as gray as stone and bristly hair on their necks and shoulders. One had a deep scar down his face that channeled rainwater from his hair across his cheek and into his mouth. He gulped and smiled up at them. Apple shivered.

"It's Her Highness!" said the goblin in a wet voice. "I told ye I felt royalty near."

"That's right," said Apple. "I am—"

"Daughter of the Great Queen herself," the goblin interrupted. He bowed to Raven. "I be Goober Fig, goblin prince. At your service, Your Dark Majesty, and so are me grubs here."

"Thank you—I mean, that's right, you will serve me," Raven said, as if trying to sound queenly. "Get us down at once."

Goober Fig shouted something in Goblinish, and his troop scrambled back inside the rock and brought out a long ladder made of bones. Animal bones, Apple assumed. Or hoped.

"What be that one?" asked a goblin, sniffing the air with a piglike snout. He pointed a clawed finger at Apple. "She does smell like sugar."

"*Hmph.* I'm Apple." She was about to say more, but Raven nudged her.

"We wants the Apple," said the goblin prince. "It looks delicious. What a stew it would make! Give us the plump red Apple."

Apple pulled her raincoat around herself tighter. She didn't mind if someone called her plump, unless that someone was imagining her in a stew.

"Um…" Raven said.

"No Apple, no ladder," he said, snarling.

"Yes, okay," said Raven. "Help us down first, and I swear I will give you what you ask."

"Raven!" said Apple.

"Ye swears on your mother's crown? Ye swears on bat wings and slug tails? Ye gives us the Apple and no zapping with magic for hurting our hides?"

"Yes, I swear it," said Raven.

The goblins cheered.

Apple felt cored. She could not believe Raven Queen would be capable of such cruelty, such selfish disregard for anyone besides herself. Well, sure, she'd been encouraging Raven to embrace her destiny, but now was a terrible time to suddenly turn evil. When they'd been singing together in the woods, Apple had actually thought…had truly believed…that she and Raven had become friends.

Apple felt her eyes get wet, and she blinked tears.

The goblins leaned the bone ladder against the cliff wall, holding it steady. Raven climbed down first.

"I'm not coming," said Apple.

"Come down," said Raven.

"No," said Apple. She was shivering. She tried to sit, but the jagged rocks poked her backside and she bolted upright.

"Trust me," said Raven, looking up. "I have some experience with goblins. It'll be all right. Come down."

Apple gulped. Raven was asking a lot.

As she climbed down the ladder, the goblins holding it steady snuffled at her arms and hair and made grunting remarks to one another in Goblinish.

As soon as Apple's feet hit rock, Raven grabbed her and put herself between Apple and the goblins. The goblins hissed.

"Your oath!" cried Goober Fig.

"You served me well, and I'll keep my oath," said Raven. She reached into her backpack and pulled out an apple. "Here's what I promised you—a plump red apple."

Apple exhaled.

Goober Fig grabbed the fruit from Raven's hand. He growled, but it turned into a laugh.

"A pleasure being tricked by Your Majesty," he said with a bow.

The other goblins laughed, too, a snarling, soggy sound. Apple tried to smile.

"It be wet. Come into our home," Goober Fig said to Raven, gesturing into the opening of the mountain. "We be honored by your visit."

"Thank you very much for your help," said Apple sweetly. "But we must be going now."

She started down the path cut into the rocky cliff. But Goober Fig snarled something, and two goblins scampered past Raven and grabbed Apple by her arms.

"Tricks or no, we be having apple stew!" Goober Fig shouted.

"Let her go or I'll—" Raven started, her hands out as if ready to cast a spell, but Apple had had enough.

"Why, how dare you!" she said. "I am Princess Apple White, daughter of Snow White and future queen. Take your hands off me at once, or I swear by wishing wells, seven-league boots, silver wands, and all marvelous things that *you will regret it*!"

The goblins backed away from her, looking uneasily at their prince.

"But…stew…" he said sadly.

"You have behaved most nobly," said Apple. "You

were princely in your rescue! At the moment, I think very well of you. Don't you want me to keep thinking well of you?"

The goblin prince sniffed. Apple smiled. And then...she batted her eyelashes.

Goober Fig stood up straighter. "Yes, princess. Thank you, princess."

"Good. What a fine, strong goblin you are. All of you. Shining specimens of goblininess. Thanks again! We must be on our way!"

Apple grabbed Raven's hand, and they ran down the rocky trail.

"You were *awesome* back there," Raven whispered.

"I do very well in Debate class," said Apple. "But *your* trick was so clever!"

"I do pretty well in General Villainy," said Raven. "Though sometimes I try to fail it."

"But failing a class is bad, Raven."

"Yeah, that's where I get confused. Which makes me less of a villain? Acing a class called General Villainy or failing it? Doomed if I do, doomed if I don't."

And suddenly, after a mostly silent journey, the

two girls couldn't stop talking. They ran down the mountainside exchanging stories: the worst thing about being a princess or villain, the best, the oddness of their instructors and advisors, their favorite kind of pie at the Three Bears Porridge Café. Fashion and music and how good it would feel to get back to their soft, warm beds again.

The rain stopped. And the stars came out.

CHAPTER 19

MADDIE ~~PESTERS~~ THE NARRATOR YET AGAIN

Narrator?

Maddie, you should be asleep.

Huh? Oh, sleep magic never works on me. I think my brain assumes I'm already asleep and real life is dreams—or are dreams real life? Anyway, I can't find Raven. I've looked everywhere—my hat, under my mattress, in the closet, behind the drapes, even in her room—

You know I'm only supposed to observe the story.

I can't tell you that she's out looking for…ack! Nothing. She's looking for nothing. Never mind.

Raven's looking for something? Something lost? That's right—she asked me about finding lost things. I'm going to help her. Right after teatime! Everyone's asleep in the kitchen, but I found some spritzle-fizzle tea made with molted lizard skin and discarded fairy wings, and it makes your taste buds sizzle and your voice sound like the happy buzz of honeybees.

Ooh, you must get me the recipe.

Absotively! I'll think it at you first thing tomorrow. Right after I find what you told me Raven lost.

But I didn't say a word about Bella Sister!

Raven is looking for someone named Bella Sister? Oh, Narrator, thank you so much for the tip!

Argh!

CHAPTER 20

Warning RED PAINT ON THE WALL

S O WHEN BRIAR GOT ME UP ON THE GREAT Beanstalk," Apple was saying, "and gave me a push, I literally thought I would die. My whole life flashed before my eyes—my first canopy bed, my first trip to the Pegasus petting zoo, the time I fell down a well...."

"It seems like hanging out with Briar can be a death-defying experience," said Raven.

"Oh, you don't know the half of it! She'd love this quest, honestly. What a kick she'd get out of dangerous cliffs and hungry goblins, and if you got her into that marsh, she'd refuse to leave till she'd persuaded the Marsh King to host a dance."

"Maddie would have thrown a tea party for the Marsh King and insisted he stand on his head and sing till he cheered up."

A curve of the moon peered through the parting clouds. Raven could see the ground beneath her at least. They were walking along the sandy bank of a stream at the bottom of a gully. Around them, mountains loomed in an enormous horseshoe. She spied dark crevasses that could hide caves, but what she wanted was the yellow sand trail Bella Sister had mentioned in the note. Raven hoped it was *really* yellow—like canary, lemon, Blondie's hair yellow—so she wouldn't miss it in the moonlight.

"I'm not normally a scaredy-pig," Apple continued, "but my heart has never beat so hard as when I bungee jumped off the Beanstalk with Briar. Or when I was six and fell down a well. Or when you told the goblins they could eat me."

"I'm sorry! I was trying to nudge you and wink at you the whole time so you'd know it was a trick."

"Oh, it's all right. I wasn't scared of a little old

troop of people-eating goblins," said Apple. "I knew I could talk them out of it."

Raven *had* been afraid with the goblins. Not just afraid they would eat Apple, though that had been frightening enough. No, she'd been afraid because she knew how to stop them. All she had to do was be regal, be commanding and terrifying, dark and magical and powerful. All she had to do was be like her mother, and they would obey her absolutely. But once she became like her mother, could she ever go back to being Raven again?

"Wait—if you weren't scared of the goblins, what were you scared of?" Raven asked.

"*Hm?* Oh, well"—Apple looked at her hands, suddenly shy—"I guess I was scared that you *wanted* to feed me to the goblins. I mean, I'm prepared to accept a poisoned apple from you, because that's part of our story. But offering up someone for goblin stew is not something, you know, traditionally, that friends do."

Raven put her arm around Apple's shoulders. "I'd like to be your friend, too."

Raven felt warm and hopeful, as if she had a bellyful of just-right porridge. They were getting closer. Surely they would find evidence of Bella

Sister's happy escape from her terrible destiny. Apple would see there was another way, and she would understand when Raven took it. To be free from the chains of her mother's choices! Raven nearly skipped past a yellow sand trail.

"Oh! A yellow sand trail!" said Apple.

Lucky at last. Everything was turning around for Raven Queen.

The trail swished and swayed this way and that, away from the stream and climbing up toward the mountain. Ahead was the opening of a cave as if the mountain had yawned. Raven imagined a cozy home built inside, where Bella and her sister settled down happily together, fishing in the stream, hunting in the woods, making friends with their goblin neighbors, and generally being free.

They had to duck when they entered the cave. Water droplets gathered on the rock ceiling, occasionally falling into a small pool.

Drip. Drip. Drip.

"This doesn't look like a place someone would come to live," Raven said, her voice echoing off stone.

The ceiling rose up farther in. They found remains of a small wooden table and chair, gnawed by termites up to its knees. The cave smelled of mold and festering things.

"Maybe Bella didn't stay long," Raven whispered. "Maybe she just waited here till her sister found her, and together they ran off to a faraway kingdom to make their own Happily Ever—"

Apple gasped.

On a moth-bitten blanket lay a skeleton, curled up on its side, still wearing a half-rotted dress.

"Is it...was that Bella Sister?" Apple asked.

Raven crouched beside the skeleton. "It could be anyone. I mean, Bella Sister lived so long ago someone else might have taken shelter in here and...and died here."

Please don't let it be her....

"Look." Apple held up a stained, decaying canvas bag she found under the fallen table. Stitched onto its pocket were the symbol of Ever After High and the name BELLA SISTER.

"Curses," said Raven. "But...wait, this means she didn't go *poof*, right?"

"Maybe that's how it works," said Apple. "*Poof*, nothing left but a skeleton."

"Maybe," said Raven.

"In the very best scenario, she lived and died alone."

"But…we don't know when she died. Maybe she lived a long life and died here naturally. Sure, she was probably cold and lonely and hungry and dirty and miserable…but maybe it was better than being evil."

Apple held up the lantern. Her eyes widened. Raven looked.

On the rock wall, written in red paint, was: I SHOULD HAVE SIGNED THE BOOK.

"No…it's a mistake," said Raven. "Bella Sister was happy. I just know it. She rebelled against the book and she was okay and she got away and…and—"

"Raven, I think it's pretty clear what happened to her."

"No!" Raven said. She was getting angry now, though there was no one to be angry with. "There's a mistake—"

"Bella Sister fled here and regretted it. Her sister never forgave her, or else she disappeared when Bella didn't sign, and when Bella found out—"

"Look!" said Raven, examining the words on the wall. "There's a gnat stuck in this paint. This was painted recently. If this really happened long ago, the gnat would have disintegrated by now."

"How are you suddenly an expert on bugs?"

"I'm the daughter of a dark sorceress, Apple. I know about these kinds of things. And I say it's fake."

"No, you *want* it to be fake," said Apple. "You're making up excuses so you don't have to believe it's true."

Raven clenched her fists. Trembling, she took a hold of her fury as if it were a rope and whipped it over her head. A dark streak cracked in the air above them, sparking like dull lightning. Immediately insects emerged from everywhere: cockroaches, spiders, black crickets, ants, termites, beetles.

"See?" said Raven. "I know bugs."

Apple's nostrils flexed. "Stop avoiding the truth! If you don't sign, our story ends. We vanish or die just like Bella and her sister, and…and, um, Raven? Raven, the, uh…the bugs…they're moving."

The floor was alive with scurrying, flicking, chittering insects. All coming toward the girls.

"Stop them," Apple said through clenched teeth, as if afraid the bugs could read lips.

"I can't. That would be a good thing, and my magic always backfires, especially when I try to do something good." The bugs kept coming, a crawling carpet with thousands of eyes. "Oh, wait, I know what we can do."

"What?" Apple said without moving her mouth.

"Run." Raven took off, Apple on her heels, screaming as a swarm of flying, crawling, leaping insects chased them.

"Aah!" Apple screamed. "Aah! I mean, *La la la*!" Apple sang desperately. "*LA LA LA LA!*"

At first there was no helpful response. But instead of running back the way they'd come over the mountain, they ran south along the stream bank. No time to find the best path. They splashed through shallows, ripped through bulrushes, tripped over rocks, and careened through weeds.

Apple kept singing, and eventually birds heard. Swarms of songbirds rushed toward Apple's call and dived at the insects. Robins pecked at spiders, bluebirds gobbled up black crickets, chickadees attacked cockroaches. Sparrows, wrens, and starlings tweeted while they munched on bugs. Soon there were no bugs left.

Raven, covered in dirt and un-princess-y sweat, fell down into a fern, gasping for breath.

"No…more…bug…spells," Apple said, leaning over to catch her breath.

Raven nodded. She felt as grimy as a goblin tongue. Her hair was loose and tangled, full of twigs and leaves. Her clothes were ripped, her stockings full of burrs, and her boots muddy.

"I'm such a mess!" said Apple.

Raven glanced at Apple and did a double take. Apple's blond hair was still lightly curled and shiny. Her clothing was somehow perfectly clean but for one dry leaf clinging to her cloak, which Apple quickly plucked off. The only sign of their flight for life was a lovely rosy glow in Apple's round cheeks.

Raven groaned and fell backward into the fern.

Apple perched on a rock beside her. "Raven, I don't want you to end up dead on some cave floor. I think she *poofed*. And so will you if you don't sign."

"Maybe."

"Your life is worth more than a false hope. You have to sign the book."

Raven sighed. "I know," she whispered.

Apple smiled her confident smile. "Don't be afraid.

You won't be alone in your story. I'll be there with you."

Raven pretended to be still too out of breath to answer. She *was* afraid. Of many things. Turning into her mother, disappointing her father, eating cooked carrots, stepping on squishy things, and, most recently, being chased by a swarm of enchanted insects. But just then what she most feared was that Apple was right.

The letter, the skeleton, Old Man Winters, the words on the wall—all the evidence was too strong for one little gnat to undo. Raven was grasping at a house of straws. No matter what she did, she was doomed. But at least by playing her part in the story, Raven had a chance to create a Happily Ever After for Apple. And Daring Charming, too. And for all the people in the world who would continue to know and love the tale of Snow White.

"I'll do it," she whispered. "I'll sign."

"Thank you, Raven," said Apple.

No relief came with the decision. Raven turned her face away from Apple and quietly cried.

CHAPTER 21

A NOTICING GAME

THE IMAGES CAME FAST AND ANGRY, LIKE A swarm of wasps stinging.

Raven, lying on the sandy ground, covered in creepy-crawlies. Spiders, cockroaches, termites, ants, crickets—they smother her, nibble on her, devouring her from hair to toenails in seconds, leaving just a skeleton behind.

Apple, standing at the podium on Legacy Day. *Poof*, she disappears. And reappears in a goblin cave. The goblin troop moves in, brandishing salad bowls and chopping knives.

Daring Charming, no story to call home, thins and melts into a wisp of a ghost, swimming endlessly through walls.

The crowded Charmitorium at Ever After High, Headmaster Grimm on the stage. "And remember, students, no matter what you do, don't follow the example of the worst, most despised, most selfish character in all of Ever After history—Raven Queen!"

"Boo!" the students yell.

"Boo!" says the Daring ghost.

Apple's head in a goblin bowl opens her eyes and looks straight at Raven. "Boo!"

RAVEN AWOKE FROM THE NIGHTMARE WITH A jerk. Her legs and feet were soaked. She sat up.

They were in a small, leaky boat floating on a lake. Apple was still asleep. The damp at the bottom of the boat had turned into a pool of water, but somehow only on Raven's side.

Apple—completely dry—stirred, stretched, and yawned prettily. Raven imagined that was how she'd wake for her prince after her poisoned-apple nap.

"How long have we been asleep?" Apple asked, rubbing her eyes under her glasses.

They'd discovered the abandoned boat on the shore around dawn. Now the sun was straight up, looking down like a Cyclops eye.

"A few hours," said Raven. "At least we're still drifting in the right direction."

Far off to the left of the lake were the goblin mountains and the marsh. Raven was relieved they wouldn't have to walk that way again.

"Water!" said Apple.

"Yeah. We're in a lake."

"Water! In the boat! I don't swim, Raven!"

In a panic, Apple began to paddle with her hands, trying to direct the boat to shore. Raven paddled, too, and they made it to the eastern shore still afloat.

It was a long trek up a hillside, but at least there were no goblins. They were too tired to talk. By the time they made it to the Village of Book End, it was evening. The street was empty, the shops closed.

In the distance, they could see the Night Briars still surrounding Ever After High. Raven led Apple to the Mad Hatter of Wonderland's Tea & Hat Shoppe.

The door was unlocked. Raven opened it, rattling a bell.

The Mad Hatter opened a round, striped door high up on a wall.

Even in his enormous felt top hat, he was only as tall as Raven. His hair was the same mint green as his daughter Maddie's, only instead of lavender streaks around his face, his was streaked with white. His prominent overbite was all the more obvious because of his constant smile.

"Hello, sir," said Raven.

"Raven!" said the Mad Hatter. "Why is a raven like a writing desk?"

"Well," said Raven, "both don't have gills."

"Ah, very good," he said.

"What are you two talking about?" Apple asked Raven, yawning behind her hand.

"It's a riddle," she whispered back. "He always asks, and I always give him a different answer."

"So wait," Apple said, sitting at a table. "Why *is* a raven like a writing desk?"

"I haven't the slightest idea," said the Mad Hatter.

"Mr. Hatter," said Raven, "we're locked out of the high school—"

"So you need a new hat," said the Mad Hatter.

"Um…"

Apple had rested her head on a saucer on the table. She emitted a gentle snore.

"Well, I never," said the Mad Hatter. "Sleeping on a saucer! Where are her manners? A proper princess would curl up in a teacup."

It turned out the Mad Hatter had an enormous teacup in the back room, filled to the brim with pillows and feather-stuffed comforters. He offered it to Apple and Raven to sleep out the night.

The next morning, they had tea and crumpets with lots and lots of fairyberry jam and walked back to Ever After High just after the briars dissolved. The rest of the school was just gathering in the Castleteria for the Beauty Sleep Festival brunch. Apple and Raven hurried up to their room to change into pajamas.

"We made it!" Apple said, taking off her glasses and putting them away in her desk.

"Yeah," said Raven. She pretended to smile.

They entered the Castleteria together and paused in the threshold. Raven wasn't sure what would happen now.

"You can sit with us, Raven," said Apple, gesturing toward the table full of princesses.

"Another time," said Raven. "I should join Maddie."

After so many hours together, it felt strange to walk away from Apple.

"Wait," said Apple. She grabbed Raven and gave her a fierce hug. "I know you'll do the right thing. I'm so happy we're truly friends now. Our story is safe!"

Raven patted Apple's back. "I'm happy to be your friend, too," she said. But she couldn't manage to be happy about much else. Her hopes for a fresh page were ripped, her future looming like a heavy tome above her head.

But she watched Apple join Briar and Blondie and felt relieved that at least Apple's Happily Ever After was definite.

"Hello, my beamish friend!" said Maddie, giving Raven a huge hug. "I've been missing you."

Raven hugged her and felt as if she got a little missing piece of herself back.

"Well, I slept like a log!" said Cedar.

"What a catnap," said Kitty Cheshire, passing by

with her tray of cheese, sardines, and a bowl of milk. She somehow managed to keep her constant smile even when yawning.

Cerise's yawn took over half her face and showed all her teeth. On her tray was a plate of sausages with a side of sausages.

"Hey, Cerise," said Cedar.

Cerise nodded and started for an empty table in the corner.

"Oh, just sit with us," said Raven. "We may be evil, mad, and wooden, but we're not half bad."

Cerise hesitated but sat down. "I don't think you're half bad. I just...I don't have very good table manners, so..."

"We don't mind," said Maddie as she sat cross-legged on the tabletop.

Cerise started in on her sausages, making growling sounds as she wolfed them down. She froze and looked up, part of a sausage hanging out of her mouth. Raven realized that she, Cedar, and Maddie were all staring.

"Sorry," Cerise mumbled with a mouth full of food.

"No, no, you're fine," Raven said.

Cerise held up her napkin to hide behind and went back to snarfing sausages. Raven looked away, pretending not to notice.

"It's okay to notice things, Raven," said Maddie. "You don't have to pretend not to."

"What?" said Raven.

"The Narrator said you were pretending not to notice something," said Maddie. "But noticing is wonderful! The Narrator's job is to notice, and I'm finding it a very helpful exercise for myself. We should play a noticing game!"

"I'm game for any Maddie game," said Raven.

"How many things can you notice that you haven't before?"

They all began to look around.

"There are twelve pillar trees in here," said Cedar. "Ooh, look at the star shapes the light makes between the leaves."

While Cedar, Cerise, and Maddie leaned back to look up, Raven noticed Cerise put a hand to her hood to keep it in place. Was she just shy? Or was she hiding something? She was set to inherit a nice fairytale, but that knowledge didn't seem to make her content. She acted as if she was an outcast.

Raven began noticing other things: the way Cerise gobbled up those sausages, her strength and speed, how pigs were afraid of her. In the same way they were afraid of wolves.

Cerise's story had a wolf, but he was her mother's villain. What could have happened—

"Does Hunter always wear that leather band on his wrist?" said Cerise.

"I'd never noticed before," said Cedar. "This game really works!"

"He's not a royal, but he always sits by them," said Cerise. "Ready to serve, I think."

Raven wondered, was it more than that? Hunter was sitting at a table beside the royals, his back to Ashlynn's. And now that Raven thought about it, he seemed to always be near Ashlynn. Raven recalled bumping into them in the Enchanted Forest, and the night both Ashlynn and Hunter were outside the school at the same time. Meeting each other?

"Whoa," said Raven. Ashlynn and Hunter were—

"Did you notice something?" said Maddie.

"Yeah," said Raven, but she didn't want to expose Ashlynn and Hunter. Any out-of-story romance was strictly forbidden and could get them expelled. "Um…look at how Duchess Swan walks. It's almost like she's dancing."

"Or gliding," said Cedar. "So graceful!"

Duchess put her tray down at the royals' table, but Raven noticed she was the only princess there who wasn't promised a Happily Ever After. Though she was the heroine and not the villain, her story ended in tragedy. Perhaps her lifted chin, her dark-eyed glare, hid sadness or fear.

Raven's attention went from face to face in the Castleteria, and she noticed for the first time just how many students at Ever After High weren't looking forward to their stories. Only no one talked about it. And the one who had dared to rebel—Bella Sister— had done so in private, running away.

So many things worth noticing. Raven could barely keep it all in her head.

When brunch was over, Maddie and Raven looked at each other. Maddie inclined her head, and Raven nodded. Both smiled. And then, at the same time, they ran.

They ran through the Castleteria, leaping over the last bench, up the central spiral stairs, through the Hall of Armor, weaving through knightly mannequins, up the secret stairs, and into Raven's room. They both collapsed, Raven on the floor and Maddie on Apple's bed.

"I won that time," said Raven. "Finally!"

"Yay for the Raven bird, watch how she flies!" Maddie laughed and started jumping on Apple's bed, the silk comforter bunching and dozens of stuffed birds and squirrels colliding into a kind of wildlife stew.

"Apple's not going to like that," said Raven.

"What a silly idea. I mean, how could Apple or anyone really mind one tiny ounce when it's *fun*? You might as well say Apple wouldn't like to be dunked in a giant cup of tea while a bluebird tap-danced on her foot and a crowd of adoring mice sang 'Mermaids Just Wanna Have Fun.'"

"Maddie, I've missed you!" said Raven. "I'm sorry I've been distracted and gone, and I've been keeping a secret from you." And she told her about her quest to uncover the fate of a character who hadn't signed. "I thought I should do it on my own so I wouldn't get anyone into trouble, and I was afraid if you or Cedar knew you might accidentally tell someone. But you're my best friend, Maddie. I should have told you from the beginning."

"It's okay." They were sitting cross-legged across from each other on Apple's bed. Maddie put her hand on Raven's knee. "I knew you'd been worried, and the Narrator told me all about it—"

I did not!

"—so I've been figuring out how to help."

"Thank you, but I don't think anyone can help. It's all over."

"But don't you want to know about the fate of Bella Sister?"

"What? How did you—when—how do you know her name?"

"Oh, well, I knew you were looking for something that was lost, and then I overheard the Narrator mention Bella Sister, so when I was in the Vault of Lost Tales, I thought, *This is the sort of place where one could find a tale that is lost, right?* So while everyone was asleep, I spent the past two days looking for a book about Bella Sister. And I think I found it! But you have to see. Come on!"

Raven thought of the time Maddie had taken Raven out of Poison Fruit Theory for an emergency that turned out to be a rock that looked like a potato.

But Maddie was standing there, her hand out, inviting, her eyes sparkling.

"Okay," said Raven.

And she ran off with her friend.

CHAPTER 22

THE U̶N̶D̶I̶S̶C̶O̶V̶E̶R̶E̶D VAULT OF LOST TALES

MADDIE HAD TAKEN RAVEN TO THE VAULT of Lost Tales once before—a labyrinth under the library inhabited by dusty books and an odd man who spoke only Riddlish. Maddie claimed he was Milton Grimm's missing brother, Giles Grimm, but Raven had a hard time believing it. Why would Headmaster Grimm's brother speak only a Wonderlandian language?

"Did you check out the book about Bella Sister?" Raven asked.

"Oh, no, there's no card catalog for the Lost Tales

and no librarian to check them out. Besides, they don't *like* to be taken. They're like a bunch of grandpas and grandmas who would rather just stay in, thank you kindly."

They entered the library, the narrow, high room like a giant's closet.

"I heard faint knocking for weeks before I was able to follow the sound here," said Maddie, pulling Raven to the dark, back side of the library. "The problem is, the entrance to the vault is always changing."

Maddie pressed her ear to a wall and knocked three times. She tried the same on a bookcase, on the floor, on a book called *How to Raise Evil Cucumbers* and another called *The History of Spitting*. She crawled on her hands and knees, knocking, then stood on chairs to knock high on walls. Raven began knocking, too, though she had no idea what she was doing.

"Maybe it's not—" Raven started to say, when the wall Maddie just knocked on suddenly swung in like a door. The two girls tumbled through.

The wall shut behind them.

Mushrooms glowed high on the walls, twinkling illumination into the dark corridor. They walked along, the way sloping down, twisting, and doubling back, a maze of hallways. The path ended at a large, heavy door with a great brass doorknob.

"This wasn't here last time," said Raven.

"The way is always different," said Maddie.

The door was locked.

"We could go get Blondie Lockes," said Raven. "That girl can unlock any door. But...I used her unlocking talent once already. I don't want her to get suspicious and tell Headmaster Grimm."

"Let me check my hat," said Maddie. She removed her Hat of Many Things and began to dig through it. "Look!"

"What?" said Raven.

"A stick!"

"Um, how does a stick help us unlock a door?"

"It doesn't. But look! A stick!" Maddie threw the stick over her shoulder and rummaged some more. "A dead fish! No, wait, it's alive—better put it back. Um...a five-leaf clover, a bowling ball, Shrinking Potion, a stunned starfish—"

"Stop!"

"You want the starfish? It is kind of cute, though a bit damp and not very entertaining, being stunned and all—"

"No, the potion. Would it shrink us?"

"Probably undoubtably! I made it in Chemythstry class."

"Maddie, you're a genius! But we'll also need a potion that will make us big again."

Maddie trolled through her hat, pulling out a pink vial of Embiggen Potion. She cocked her ear. "Yep, the Narrator said this pink vial is Embiggen Potion, so it must be. Thank you, Narrator!"

Argh! I did it again!

"Ah, so helpful, this Narrator. Yes, you are the sweeties."

Raven unthreaded a fiber from her skirt and tied it to the doorknob, letting it fall to the floor. Once they shrank, the thread would serve as a rope.

Raven grimaced at the slurpy liquid. Potions reminded her too much of her mother. But she crossed her fingers and took a sip.

The tingles started in her belly and shot outward, reaching her fingertips and toes and rising up in her nose with a smell of hot, buttered toast.

"Here, quick," Raven said, managing to shove the vial into Maddie's hand before the shrinking started. It felt like jumping off the castle roof into a pile of hay. Even though her feet never left the ground, she seemed to fall a long, long way through freezing air.

She fell down on her backside, her entire body fitting neatly inside the knothole of a floorboard. She was relieved to see her clothes had shrunk with her.

"Aww," said Giant Maddie, leaning over. Her huge face peered at Tiny Raven. Her nose was the perfect size if Tiny Raven was looking for a dance partner. "You are so adorable I just want to put you in my pocket and give you kisses and dress you in little dolly clothes and feed you minimarshmallows in thimble bowls."

"You're HUGE!" squeaked Tiny Raven. "Come join me!"

Maddie drank, *squeeeeee*ing as she shrank down beside Raven.

As Raven had suspected, there wasn't enough room beneath the door to crawl through. They'd have to go through the keyhole.

In her wee-bitty hands, the thread felt like thick rope. She clung to it, climbing the door with pushes from her wee-bitty feet. She'd had a lot of practice climbing the ivy up to her dorm-room window. But still, the muscles in her arms burned.

"This is fun!" squeaked a teeny-weeny Maddie.

At the top, Raven scrambled onto the doorknob. When Maddie was up, Raven pulled the thread up from the floor and shoved it through the brass arch of the keyhole before clambering through herself. On the other side, she let the thread fall, and she and Maddie climbed back down.

The Embiggen Potion tasted like melted peppermint ice cream. With a *whoosh*, Raven shot back up to her natural height.

"Wahoo!" said Maddie, big again, too. "Again!"

"First the book?" Raven said.

"Book, right!"

The Vault of Lost Tales was a narrow room that zigged and zagged, every wall covered in bookshelves, and nearly every bit of floor stacked with teetering book towers. The room was lit by dozens of smoky candles. Cobwebs on the ceiling twitched in a draft.

At a cluttered desk near the end of the room sat the odd, little man Maddie called Giles Grimm, hunched over a book and muttering to himself. If he really was Milton Grimm's brother, there was little family resemblance. Where the headmaster was tall and well kept, Giles was short and disheveled. His white-streaked gray hair was long and thick like a lion's mane, his beard rested on his chest, and his jacket was patched and spilling loose threads at the cuffs and hem.

"Maddie, where's the book about Bella Sister?" Raven whispered, not wanting to disturb the man.

Maddie browsed a shelf, plucked a book as if picking a flower, and handed it to Raven.

Raven turned the book over in her hands. The green leather cover was cracked and chipping, the pages yellow with age. She opened to the page marked with a ribbon. Her breath caught. "The Two Sisters." Maddie had found the lost fairytale!

Raven read about the Beautiful Sister who was so cruel, flies were drawn to her and constantly buzzed around her head. The Ugly Sister was so kind, butterflies followed her everywhere and curled up in her hair like jeweled pins. One day at the well, the Beautiful Sister had the Ugly Sister lower her into the water in order to drown the buzzing flies. After coming out, she was grumpy to be so cold and wet. She wanted the Ugly Sister to suffer, too, so she pushed her into the water. The Ugly Sister wept that the butterflies in her hair had drowned.

"Pull me out, please," the Ugly Sister begged.

But the Beautiful Sister said, "Having to see your ugly face every day is as annoying as buzzing flies," and wouldn't lower the rope.

The Ugly Sister slipped under the water, but was caught by the ghosts of her butterflies. They flew her out, and with a flash of butterfly magic, she became as beautiful in face as she was of heart. Her cruel sister became hideous to behold and was chased far away by the ghosts of the flies.

Raven read the tale aloud to Maddie. And then she read the messages two people had jotted down in the margins of the pages.

I don't want to be the mean Beautiful Sister, and I don't want to drown my awesome little sister, Brutta, so I am not going to do it! Besides, she's not ugly and that's just mean to call someone that hateful word. We found a spell that will change our well into a portal. By the time anyone finds this note, we'll be long gone into another world where we're not forced to relive stupid stories.

That's right! Besides, like I'd ever let my sister drown my pet butterflies. I regularly whip her butt in Grimmhastics class.

You wish! I'll race you to the well!

"But...but I found Bella Sister's skeleton," said Raven. "And her note in the tree. If this is true, then all that wasn't, and if all that was true—"

"Feathers and friends, together alone, the count of two, on a MirrorPhone," said a deep voice at her elbow.

Raven startled. The odd, little man stood there with a distracted smile, his mismatched socks pulled up over his pant legs.

"Excuse me?" Raven asked.

"Giles Grimm only speaks Riddlish, remember?" said Maddie. "He's just saying that it's nice to have us here again."

"Oh, right." Raven showed him the Two Sisters tale. "Is this true? Did Bella and Brutta choose to not sign the Storybook of Legends? Did they survive?"

Maddie translated Raven's questions into Riddlish.

Giles Grimm nodded. "Never, forever, tomorrow, today. Apart of together ever after away."

"He said they lived happily far away," said Maddie. "At least, I think he did. Either that or they died sadly far away. Riddlish isn't an exact language, you know."

"Which do *you* think he meant?" Raven asked.

"The first," said Maddie. "I think. Almost probably."

Raven took a deep breath. If Giles Grimm was right, then everything she'd found on the quest—the Lost and Crowned box, the letter in the tree, the skeleton and message in red paint—was fake. But who would fake all that and why? Raven's dream of escaping her mother's legacy had been squashed like a pumpkin. But the seeds of that pumpkin were slowly starting to sprout in her again.

She and Giles Grimm sat on the floor and talked for hours, Maddie's bubbly voice translating back and forth. Some of what he said, Maddie just couldn't understand.

"Riddlish is riddled with riddles, after all," said Maddie. "If it were clear, it wouldn't be Riddlish!"

"Two tools," Giles said, "one for weeds, one for woods, none with ease. A day is not destined, a lock needs no keys."

"He said, 'Legacy Day is a hoax, and the Storybook of Legends holds no real power!'" said Maddie. "Or maybe he said, 'Legacy Day is hilarious, and the Storybook of Legends is a monster.'"

"On a wing with a rose, on a chair if it chose, with a puppy and pig in its pocket."

"I know this one! He's said it to me before. It means 'Raven can change her path, as well as the path of others like her, by claiming her own Happily Ever After,'" said Maddie.

"If that is true…it changes everything!" Raven paused. She tilted her head at Maddie. "Or maybe it means…"

Maddie stuck out her bottom lip and blew a strand of lavender-colored hair out of her eyes. "Or maybe it means 'Raven can change her height and the heights of others like her by wearing high heels.'"

Giles Grimm stared at Raven, his eyes intense and intelligent. He couldn't really be talking about wearing high heels, could he? No, she believed

Maddie's first translation, though she knew what Apple would say: *You believe it because you want to believe it, not because it's true.*

If what Maddie translated was accurate, and if Giles Grimm knew what he was talking about, then Raven could choose not to sign without dooming herself or Apple.

That was a lot of *if*s.

Raven wished she knew for sure which story of Bella and Brutta was true. Whatever they'd done, they'd done it quietly, fleeing in secret and only speaking of their rebellion in the quiet margins of a long-lost book. If they had rebelled, no one knew. Except three oddballs on the floor of an underground library.

CHAPTER 23

~~The Horrible~~ *Beautiful*

THE ~~HORRIBLE~~
POWER OF EVIL

LEGACY DAY DAWNED WEAK AS WATERY porridge. Outside Raven and Apple's window, Night Briars blocked the sunlight.

The mirror on the wall blinked on. Milton Grimm's smiling face appeared.

"Good morning, students," he said. "Forgive this unscheduled Mirrorcast. You may have noticed that the Night Briars are still standing. I decided to allow the briars to remain throughout this crucial day, an added protection for all of you. Nothing can be allowed to interrupt today's Legacy Day ceremony."

He doesn't want anyone running away, like Bella and Brutta Sister did, Raven thought. *That is, if they did run away*, she reminded herself.

She watched as the briars thickened, grew longer thorns, twined extra branches. Even Hunter's ax might not make it through that thicket. Raven *had* considered running away from the choice, but no. She would choose one path, and she'd make the choice today.

"What a glorious day!" Apple said, standing beside Raven before the open window. She bent down to pet her bunny slippers. They weren't real bunnies, of course, but Apple couldn't seem to help herself. "I can't believe that after all these years of waiting, we finally have our Legacy Day! Raven, thank you for allowing me to journey with you and help prove how important today is. For all of us."

Raven smiled, but she felt sick. She couldn't really betray Apple's trust. Could she?

All the cuckoo clocks in the castle went off at once. *Coo-coo! Coo-coo! Coo-coo!*

"It's time!" Apple said, clasping her hands to her chest.

Time to get dressed. Each Legacy Day participant

would wear their heirloom outfit, the clothes that his or her fairytale parent had made famous. Raven would be literally stepping into her mother's shoes.

She shivered.

"Let's get ready together, okay?" said Apple. "I can help you do your hair and—"

There was a knock at the door.

Raven opened it to a knee-high goblin.

"Raven Queen, your heirloom dress awaits in the cauldron room," he said with a squeak.

"Figures," said Raven.

She waved good-bye to Apple and followed the goblin. Instead of taking the stairs, he led her to a cupboard in the back of the enormous kitchen. Behind the cupboard door was an opening and the beginning of a black metal slide.

"Is this the garbage chute?" she asked.

The goblin smiled, showing three teeth. "If it is, then garbage has all the fun."

He pushed off and slid away.

Raven hesitated till she heard the goblin's distant "wahoooo!"

She crawled into the cupboard, sat, and let herself fall.

The slide dipped immediately straight down, stealing all her breath. Then came a rise and another drop. Her stomach felt full of ghost butterflies, tingly and ticklish. She lifted her hands and yelled, "Wahooo!"

The slide brought her feetfirst into the castle's dungeon level. The cauldron room was as wide as a sports field. In the center sat the massive metal cauldron, bubbling with the molten lava that heated the school. It was Mr. Badwolf's preferred classroom and contained the treasure vault for all villains. Also, it was a little muggy. She was glad she was wearing short sleeves.

A troop of castle goblins surrounded an upright iron coffin. With clippers taller than they were, three goblins snipped through a chain. The coffin door swung open.

Inside on a wire dummy stood her mother's dress. Raven remembered it from her childhood, the special-occasion dress her mother put on when playing hostess to evil fairies, giants, sorceresses, and the most prestigious of witches.

It was a black that when moving reflected silver and purple tones. The bodice was built like armor, the skirts wide and fearless. Daggers jutted from the sleeves at the elbows, spikes at the shoulders.

One by one, the goblins bowed to her and left, shutting the cauldron-room door with an ominous thud. Raven was alone in the dim, hot room. She put on her mother's dress.

She was expecting the dress to hang loose on her or hug too tight across the hips. But it fit her like a glove. She put on the gloves, and even the gloves fit like a glove. No part scratched or pinched. Perfect. As if the dress had been made just for her. The Evil Queen was who Raven was born to be.

She took it off quickly, letting it pool on the floor.

"I won't wear it," she whispered. "I won't be her."

She would just wear the clothes she'd put on that morning—a shimmery purple top with metal chain belts, purple leggings, and black knee-high boots with silver studs.

But she did hook on her mother's cape. It was a wicked-awesome cape, with a high collar and fabric that shimmered and captured the glance. And she put on the crown, an intricate silver dome with purple jewels dripping onto her forehead. She was a Queen, after all. She didn't want to become her mother, but she couldn't completely deny her legacy. No matter what choice she'd make today.

"I don't want to sign," she whispered under the bubble of the great cauldron.

But if she didn't, she was risking her entire life—and possibly Apple's, too—on wonderful but mad Maddie and her riddle-spouting, lost librarian. How could she be certain which path to take?

"*Follow the river to the woods and take the path on the right,*" she sang to herself as she sat at a vanity of carved ebony.

Raven rarely wore makeup. That required mirror-staring, a hobby she wanted to leave to her mother. The vanity's silver mirror was wet with humidity. Makeup in tarnished silver cases was laid out on the tabletop.

"*Take the right path that won't end in a bath, the path that leads through the night,*" she sang, darkening her lids and under-eyes with dragon-blue-green shadow. She drew on dramatic dark pink lips. She sculpted her brows.

"Wicked awesome," she whispered at her own reflection.

When she left the cauldron room, a goblin cellar worker was sweeping the dank corridor.

"Your Majesty," he rasped in awe, bowing till his forehead touched the stone ground.

Other goblins poked their heads out of the catacombs and closets. As she walked, creatures followed behind her. Goblins, a swarm of bats, large rats skittering on long claws, two lumbering trolls dragging wooden clubs, and a blue-skinned ogre with a scar across one eye.

Magic tingled in Raven's fingertips. There was power in the shadows, and it was pulsing, waiting to aid her.

She emerged in the main hallway of the school, afternoon light streaming in through the windows. The students of Ever After High were lining up to get good seats on the terrace for the Legacy Day ceremony. But it was not the Evil Queen's legacy to wait in line.

No one screamed. No one spoke. They just knew to make way for her, pressing against the walls, eyes averted, shaking in her presence.

Raven felt awesome.

She walked down the cleared aisle, her horde of followers grunting, scraping, flapping, and scampering behind her. She knew they would do whatever she asked of them. If she said, "Tear this building to the ground!" they would squeal with joy.

She finally got what her mother meant about the power of evil. And how beautiful it could be.

There was Duchess Swan, who in nursery-rhyme school used to tell the other students not to play with Raven because she ate spiders for breakfast. And Headmaster Grimm, who was always trying to force her to do things she didn't want to do. And Sparrow Hood, who had taped a KICK ME, I'M EVIL sign to her back at a picnic when they were eight. And there were the Merry Men, who had done what the sign said.

She could snap her fingers, and the creatures at her back would hunt out every person who had made Raven feel like trash and throw them into the river. And maybe she would. Maybe this was the right path after all. Maybe being the Evil Queen wouldn't be so bad!

"Raven?"

Raven turned. For a flash, she felt the words on

her tongue: *Who dares address the queen by her name?* But she swallowed them.

It was Dexter. He was wearing a gray wool jacket with gold embellishments, a deep blue cloak, and a full crown. But he still had on his blue jeans and high-top sneakers.

"Raven, is that really you?" He approached her, walking around a clump of first-year students who were huddled on the floor, cowering with their arms over their heads. "Whoa, you look...well, you look *really* different. Than normal. I mean, you look nice, the whole"—he gestured to his eyes and mouth—"and the whole"—he gestured to his own crown and cape. "Like, *way* fancy. But seriously, I almost didn't recognize you. And you looked so angry!" He laughed. "Awesome, though, for real. But...are you okay?"

"I..." Was she okay? Just a moment ago, she'd been feeling better than okay. She'd been feeling wicked powerful.

"Hey, did you know you've got, like, an army of creatures behind you? Is this the kind of stuff you do in dark-sorcery classes? Because in Hero Training, we don't get minions or anything. Anyway, I'm glad

I found you. I know this is a weird day for everyone, but especially for you, and I just wanted to tell you—I don't know—good luck, I guess, for whatever that's worth. And ... and I hope whatever you see when you open the book—your story—that it's a good one, you know?"

"Thanks, Dex," she said. "You too."

"Raven!" Maddie came skipping up. She was wearing a blue-and-gold suit with a purple cravat, but she'd updated her outfit, fitting the jacket at the waist, shortening the pants into cute capris, and adding a sparkly skirt overlay on top. Her mint-and-lavender hair was full of curls and fell all to one side, a purple top hat tipped to the other. She leaned close and whispered, "Are you ready? Do you know what you're going to do?"

"Not completely," said Raven. "But I know what to do next."

She took a deep breath. Being the Evil Queen wouldn't be a part-time job. If she was the type of girl who commanded ogres and goblins to toss Headmaster Grimm and Duchess Swan into the river, she couldn't also be the type of girl who hung out with Maddie and Cedar, singing karaoke and painting one another's nails. Besides, Dexter thought she was good. She didn't want to let him down.

Raven turned to face her minion horde. Their eyes lit up with pure adoration just to see her face, and they began to shake with glee. She lifted her hands, and those with knees fell onto them, all eyes seeming to plead for a command. Whatever task she gave them they would execute happily.

But she said, "Thanks, I really do appreciate it. But I'm not who you think I am."

"You are," a goblin growled. "But you are, Majesty."

Raven just turned and walked away.

CHAPTER 24

BORN TO WEAR IT
Perfectly!

AFTER RAVEN LEFT THEIR ROOM, APPLE stood alone at the window, waiting. Her mother had told her, "On Legacy Day, your heirloom dress will come to you." Or rather, she'd squeaked it. Apple adored her mother, but she had to admit, she sounded a great deal like a chipmunk.

Apple was expecting a flock of songbirds to fly over the briars carrying the dress. Instead she heard *tip-tapp*ing steps come down the hall.

An antlered head pushed open the door and a family of deer entered her room—stag, doe, and fawn. They bowed their heads. Apple curtsied in return. Deer were extremely polite animals. The fawn approached, clothing draped across its back. Its large, dark eyes gazed up at Apple in adoration.

"Thank you," said Apple, taking the gown and cape. *How odd*. Did the deer have some sort of clothes closet out in the woods? Ah well, it didn't matter. So many magical surprises for the future Snow White!

She took the white shoes off the fawn's ears and gave its fuzzy head a rub. It stretched its neck and touched its wet black nose to hers, its eyes seeming to say, "You are the hope of all things good and pure."

After bidding the deer farewell, Apple put on her dress. The white top was quilted and fitted, while the full red skirt exploded from the golden belt at her hips and made her want to twirl. Her quilted cape clasped around her neck with three strings of pearls.

Apple was sorry Raven had dashed off to the dungeons. It would have been so appropriate to finish getting ready with her roommate, new friend, and future nemesis. Instead, she climbed to the highest tower of the dorms, where Rapunzel's daughter lived.

Holly O'Hair's twin sister, Poppy, who was the stylist at the Tower Salon, was lending her talents for Legacy Day princess prep. Where Holly's auburn hair flowed to the ground, Poppy had cut hers stylishly short and dyed it a fierce purple. She was threading her sister's hair with ribbons and flowers.

Apple modeled her dress for Briar and Blondie.

"Mirror, mirror on the walls, who's the fairest in the halls?" said Briar. "You are, Apple White!"

"Thanks," Apple said, lowering her head modestly.

Apple suspected Briar had updated her mother's gown a bit. Briar's heritage dress was hot pink and black, the skirt sporting an asymmetrical cut. Her cape sparkled with a rose-and-thorn print and a fancy ruffled collar. Her ever-present crownglasses were tucked behind her silver-and-pink rosebud tiara.

"You look fairy pretty! You too, Blondie," said Apple, admiring the girl's canary-yellow gown and periwinkle cape with faux bear fur trim.

"Here, let me fix you up," said Poppy. She put a twist into the top of Apple's hair and pinned her delicate golden crown over it.

"Seriously, Apple, you are going to look rocking

at the dance tonight in that spellbinding dress," said Briar.

"It does feel like I was born to wear it!"

The girls snapped photos of one another and uploaded them to MyChapter. Apple updated her status: *This is going to be a perfect day!*

The princesses were the last to arrive on the Legacy Day terrace. Apple thought that was fitting. After all, Cinderella had made the best impression when she sashayed into that ballroom a little bit late.

The terrace was set up with hundreds of chairs for the audience. The first-years watched with wide, hopeful eyes. The third- and fourth-years seemed smug, remembering their own Legacy Day. The faculty in the front rows mostly bore stern expressions, reminding all that this was a solemn ceremony. But Madam Maid Marian waved to her princesses. Her cone hat obscured the view for everyone unfortunate enough to sit behind her.

The second-years were lining up before the great pedestal in the order Headmaster Grimm had chosen.

"Daring! I'm so happy I'll be signing after you," said Apple, then turned to Raven. "And you right after me, Raven. Perfect!" Raven looked so much like an Evil Queen—frown and all—Apple just knew everything was going to work out.

"Yes, very appropriate," said Daring. "All the Snow White characters together."

"On Legacy Day and forever after." Apple took a deep breath and smiled. *Perfect!*

After the headmaster's riveting introduction, Cedar Wood was the first student to take the stairs. No hesitation in her wooden step. She nearly sprang to the podium, shouting out her words. Apple knew Cedar was eager to sign and get closer to her story. Her Happily Ever After would turn her into a real girl.

Next Ashlynn walked up the stairs. Apple expected the princess to exhibit the same eagerness, but her steps were slow. The large mirrors hanging from posts around the pedestal broadcast images of Ashlynn's face to the audience. But the mirrors didn't show the book, so Apple couldn't see Ashlynn's "flash-forward" story, just Ashlynn's face as she watched it. Her expression was nervous, hopeful, and then...then sad. How could she be sad? Her story ended joyously! It was almost as if Ashlynn had been hoping to see something or someone in her story who didn't show.

Ashlynn took the pen and closed her eyes as she quickly signed.

Apple frowned. She'd prefer to see the other royals being a good example of enthusiasm for this important occasion.

Daring Charming was next, and he would show everyone the proper way to wholeheartedly embrace one's destiny!

Apple turned to smile at Raven, but Raven still didn't smile back. No reason to worry. Apple knew Raven would do the right thing. She was part of something bigger than herself. They all were. Another generation would believe in goodness, in kindness, and in love conquering all—even death and poisoned apples—because Apple and Raven were willing to retell the story.

A good story was more important than anything, Apple believed. Even than one person's life.

Daring signed, and the audience cheered.

Now is my moment, Apple thought.

With her mother's cape draped over her back and a golden crown on her head, Apple already felt like the queen she would one day become. She took the steps slowly, savoring each moment. She could hear whispers from the audience.

"It's Apple White's turn!"

"She looks perfect, doesn't she?"

"Absolutely perfect!"

Her heels clicked on the red stone stairs. Her strings of pearls clinked together like wind chimes. The weight of the crown on her head felt comforting.

When Apple reached the podium, the audience began to cheer. She waved to the crowd in just the way she'd often practiced in front of a mirror. Legacy Day was the day she began her journey toward becoming a queen, the role she was born to play.

"I am Apple White, daughter of Snow White, and I am ready to pledge my destiny."

She held out her hand, and a key spun into existence above it, slowing to lie down on her palm. The touch of the cold metal felt like a kiss. When she pressed the key into the lock, the book began to change. The dark, cracked leather soaked up a red color. The Ever After High crest in the center blinked out, replaced by a red apple.

Apple held her breath. The book knew her! A warm thrill in her chest confirmed that she was doing the right thing.

She turned the key thirty degrees to the right, and the book flipped open, landing right on her page. The picture of her animated, and she watched herself play out her part in the Snow White story. It was even better than she imagined! Those adorable dwarves, such wee-little beds. Aww…

Well, Raven as the Evil Queen unnerved her a hair. She wasn't used to seeing hate in Raven's eyes. A small doubt wormed into Apple's core. But she quickly smiled it away. She would just have to accept that her friend Raven would become evil. For the good of the story.

After handsome and dashing Prince Daring woke her from her sleep, the words THEY LIVED HAPPILY EVER AFTER danced across the page.

Apple then looked up at the mirror floating before the podium and watched her reflection transform into a picture of herself years older. She looked so much like her mother, only blond. Baba Yaga wouldn't approve, but Apple did.

And so did Ever After High.

As she signed her page, the audience's cheers filled her like sand in a jar. She couldn't see a blasted thing without her glasses, but she imagined the entire crowd smiling up at her, adoration in their eyes. The sound softened that small worry about Raven. All would work out for the best. After all, that's how the story was written.

CHAPTER 25

GOING Way OFF SCRIPT

RAVEN PLODDED UP THE PEDESTAL'S STAIRS. She wanted to trust what Giles Grimm had claimed (in Riddlish), but could she? Was the risk too great? Was a story more important than any one person?

Raven kept climbing.

Across from Raven on the stairway going down, Ashlynn looked as if she'd swallowed a pumpkin whole. Regret seemed to stream from her in dark streaks. She gazed at Hunter, who waited his turn behind Raven, her chin quivering, her eyes full of perfect princess tears.

Ashlynn and Hunter. Secretly, helplessly in love.

Raven shook her head. This was cruel! Requiring teenagers to give up on their own dreams, to condemn them to the same lives as their parents. Even trapping them in the good stories was unkind. What kind of a life had no choices?

Raven felt her mother's cape billow around her with each step, and she imagined her own mother walking up these steps years ago. Had she been hesitant to become the Evil Queen, too? Even if she had, she'd signed the Storybook of Legends anyway. Raven had seen her signature in the Storybook of Legends that day in Grimm's office.

Wait! Her mother had signed to be the Evil Queen in the Snow White story. So when she'd gone off script and tried to take over other stories, the binding magic of the book should have stopped her. But it didn't. There was proof that the Storybook of Legends worked differently from what Milton Grimm had said.

It was a hoax, Giles Grimm had said.

Raven looked at Milton Grimm sitting in the

front row, arms folded, so smug with his absolute control.

Apple was waving to the audience, who were still on their feet, cheering for her. Raven made the short but surprisingly difficult trip up the last two stairs to the top of the pedestal.

"I'm so proud of you," Apple said, squeezing Raven's hand before moving away from the podium.

Raven sighed and stepped up to the podium. The cheers died as if someone had flipped the off switch. She'd never felt so watched. Her feet felt like blocks of ice.

"I am Raven Queen, daughter of the Evil Queen." Her voice reverberated against the stone castle. "And I pledge—I pledge—"

Apple was gazing up at her, full of confidence and friendly adoration. Everything would be so much easier if she just went along with what Apple wanted, what Headmaster Grimm wanted. Just played her part.

Raven gulped. She took a steadying breath.

"I am Raven Queen, and I am ready to pledge my destiny."

In the air before her, a key appeared. Gunmetal

gray and bruise purple. She took it from the air and felt the cold of the metal burn her fingers. She slid it into the keyhole and turned.

The book lunged open to the page bearing her name, but now it was illustrated with a picture of herself as she appeared even then on Legacy Day.

The picture animated. Raven saw herself gazing into a mirror, nothing so important in the world as her own face, her own singular beauty. As her mother used to do. Fast-forward to a castle, mirrors, magic spells, a poisoned apple, Apple biting, her face even paler and her lips blue, weeping dwarves, and Raven herself laughing, laughing, as if it were all a hilarious joke.

Apparently, her destiny was no longer just the Snow White story, because the book showed Raven overreaching, just as her mother had. Raven pushed aside the Bad Fairy in Sleeping Beauty's story to show her how it's done. Nevermore became a terrifying dragon at her command, and together they attacked the young prince who tried to break into the sleeping castle. The rush of power she felt was intoxicating. She reached into more stories, trying to destroy more lives, to enslave as many people as she could, so they could hurt as much as she did. If Raven couldn't have freedom, then no one should!

Raven looked up from the book to the small mirror suspended before the podium. She saw her reflection, eyes uncertain and afraid, begin to change. Now her reflection was a picture of herself many years older, her eyes full of hate. She looked beautiful and so much like her mother she got chills.

That's not who I want to be, Raven thought. *That's not who I am.*

Anger boiled up in Raven. She didn't like feeling trapped, as when her mother used to lock her in her room as punishment for being kind. Grimm was just like her own mother, trying to force her to be evil. There had to be a better way.

Raven looked at Ashlynn again, chin quivering. And Hunter, who stood stiffly on the stairs below, waiting for his turn to condemn himself to a story in which his love for Ashlynn was forbidden. And Cerise, hunched over, whatever she was hiding making her an outcast in this world of perfection and destiny.

Raven's eyes lingered on Maddie for confidence. Maddie gave her a huge smile and a thumbs-up.

Earl Grey, the dormouse, sat up on her shoulder and waved.

Raven put her shoulders back and lifted her chin—the proper Legacy Day posture, just as Headmaster Grimm had taught. She felt a kind of confidence she'd never known—not like the Evil Queen confidence of a dark sorceress backed by her minion army. No, it was a Raven Queen kind of confidence—a girl who suddenly knew that the choice she was about to make was the right one. After all, she realized, choice itself was the most powerful kind of magic.

"I am Raven Queen, and I will write my own destiny. My Happily Ever After starts now!"

With the pen she crossed out her page, two thick, inky strokes. And for good measure, she ripped the page free. The tearing of paper sounded like a new beginning.

CHAPTER 26

TREADING WATER IN A WELL

RAVEN TORE OUT HER PAGE WITH A SOUND of all hope and light vanishing. With the rip, magic exploded out from the book in a burst of hot yellow sparks. The projection mirrors shattered, silvery glass shards exploding over the edge of the terrace. The wall of Night Briars crumbled and fell, and sunlight poured in.

And Apple screamed.

All over the terrace, princesses were screaming and pinching themselves to make sure they were still there. Princess Darling Charming fainted and was caught by no fewer than twelve ready boys, who began to kick one another's shins to try to get the others to let go.

"I've got her!"

"No, I've got her!"

Apple stopped screaming but couldn't stop shaking. She stared at her hands, waiting to see them disappear. Her story depended on Raven becoming the Evil Queen. Her life depended on her story being told. Yet Raven had refused. And torn her page! There was no going back, no hope, no story, no . . . no Snow White? No Apple White? Never after again?

Panic rose up inside Apple's chest, choking her. Was she dying? Was she already dead?

"Daring!" she yelled, shaking him. "Daring, you have to save me! You have to save everyone! You're a prince! It's what you do!"

"What?" Daring drew his sword, unsure. Apple had never seen him unsure before. "What's happening? Should I fight Raven?"

More screaming.

"We're all dead! We're all going to die!"

"She tore the book!"

"She tore our destinies!"

Daring started toward the pedestal, where Raven still stood, the torn page in her hand, shattered mirrors raining glass behind her. She looked not like an Evil Queen just then—not scary and mean and proud. She did look a little afraid, but also…also relieved. And confident. Brave, even. Like a hero at the end of a quest.

No, more than that, Apple thought. Raven looked like a queen.

Apple's chin trembled. By refusing to be evil, Raven had committed the greatest evil of all time.

"I didn't disappear," Raven said, hugging herself as if to make sure. She looked at Headmaster Grimm. "You lied! I didn't disappear!"

Daring was climbing the stairs, his sword in his hand.

"Wait!" Apple went after him, pulling on his jacket. "Stop, Daring. You can't fight her!"

"What do I do now, Raven?" asked Hunter, next in line.

"I don't know," said Raven. "Do whatever you need to do. Sign if you want. Or don't."

"But…but…" Hunter looked at Ashlynn, who

was freely crying, then at Apple, the princess he was supposed to help in his destined story.

"I'm sorry," said Raven. She faced the muddle of second-year students, who had been waiting for their turn to sign. "I'm not trying to tell you what to do. I just couldn't do it for myself. But if you don't want to sign, I don't think you have to. Nobody *poofed*! We *can* choose for ourselves!"

"No!" said Apple, hurrying back up the steps. "Don't listen to her! She destroyed my story, but she can't be allowed to destroy yours, too! You must sign—all of you *must sign*!" Apple was sobbing. She reached the final step and pushed Raven aside, leaning over the podium to call out at the audience. "Please don't throw away the stories! Don't turn your backs on your destinies! She's wrong."

"But Apple—" Raven started.

"That is *enough*!" Milton Grimm, who had been frozen in a kind of shocked stupor, now shook himself to anger. He stomped up the pedestal and seized the Storybook of Legends, holding it tight to his chest. "Never in all my decades have I witnessed such callous, such wanton, such vile behavior! Clearly this class isn't ready to make intelligent choices, so you lose your choice altogether! Legacy Day is canceled!"

The headmaster, hugging the book, hurried down the steps and ran back inside the castle, the faculty following him.

Chaos erupted anew. Some wails of disappointment turned to anger. But Apple was surprised to hear amid the ruckus some cheers growing. Cheers of relief.

Apple turned to Raven, her cheeks flushed a Red Delicious hue. "How could you be so selfish? If you don't take your part in the story, you're stealing my Happily Ever After. You're hurting everyone!"

The screams of terror built and built till Apple could no longer hear her own worried breathing. Raven covered her ears.

Raven faced the audience and thrust out her hands. "Hold everything!"

There was a burst of blue.

The next thing Apple knew, warm tingles skated down her limbs. Raven had frozen everyone on the terrace, unfreezing Apple alone.

"I didn't know I could do that," Raven whispered, looking at her hands.

"Raven…" Apple could barely speak.

"I'm sorry, Apple, but I don't want anyone to tell me who I have to be. I want to figure that out on my own. And look—if I didn't *poof*, then no one will, right? I think we can all choose our own destiny. Including you."

"I liked the destiny I had! But because of you, now it might not happen. And...*think*? You were willing to risk your life, mine, *everyone's*, on what you *think*? Well, *I* think you're wrong. And I'm...I'm scared, Raven...." Apple's sobs drowned out her words.

"So am I. But, Apple, this could be really great. Choice means you can still choose to be Snow White. What did you tell me once? The story will work itself out." Raven held out her hand. "Let's see what happens next. Together? Please?"

Apple shivered. Raven wasn't just asking her to come along on a quick journey over marshes and goblin-infested cliffs. That quest had only taken two days. Raven was asking Apple to give up all known paths forever after. To lose everything that was known and safe. To spend her *entire life* on unfamiliar paths and wind-beaten cliffs. Every day uncertain, dangerous, treading water in a well with no guarantee of a Happily Ever After.

Raven was asking too much.

"What you did, Raven...I can't even look at you...."

Apple turned and ran.

She couldn't go to her room. Raven might go there. She thought of running to the Enchanted Forest. But sorrow and uncertainty exhausted her. She barely managed to climb the stairs to the dorms and shuffled into Briar's room. She felt confident Briar would look for her there as soon as Raven unfroze everyone.

Though maybe Raven wouldn't unfreeze them, since she was apparently evil now. Though not evil in the way she was *supposed* to be evil.

The first one to find her was Gala.

The snow fox must have left the Enchanted Forest the moment Raven didn't sign, zipping straight to Apple. Could the creature sense her distress from afar? Gala leaped into her arms and snuggled against her neck. Apple sighed.

"Here she is!" Briar shouted from the doorway. "I've found her!"

Briar grabbed Apple and gave her several tight squeezes. "We thought you'd *poofed* because Raven destroyed your story! You were there one second and gone the next. Maddie said Raven froze us and you left while we were frozen, but who can believe anything Maddie says? Oh, Apple, I'm so sorry!"

And then Briar's room was filled with people.

"I've got you!" Daring said heroically, picking Apple up.

"I didn't faint, Daring," Apple protested. "You can put me down."

"I've got her!" Daring shouted. "I've saved her!"

Daring placed her on a chaise lounge.

"That was a grotesque display by Raven Queen!" said Duchess.

"Not just right," said Blondie. "Not just right at all."

"Raven Queen destroyed Legacy Day," said Daring. "Well, at least *I* was able to sign."

"Off with their heads!" Lizzie Hearts shouted, red-faced and stomping. "Off with *all* their heads!"

Apple supposed it was a good thing that Lizzie Hearts didn't have any minions to carry out her orders or there would be daily beheadings.

"Did you hear the cheers?" Briar asked. "Actual cheers! I didn't know there were so many rebels at Ever After High. I...I..." Briar's eyes closed.

Daring caught her before she hit the floor in a sudden nap. He placed her on another chaise lounge. There was no shortage of chaise lounges in Briar's room.

"Those *rebels*!"

"They ruined everything!"

"Our Legacy Day stolen!"

"Will the dance be canceled, too?"

"We need to do something!"

"Enough with the huffing and puffing," Apple said, straightening up. She had to stop moping. This was just the sort of calamity that a queen should be able to handle. "What happened *was* terrible, but Headmaster Grimm...well, he's Headmaster Grimm. And he'll take care of it. Everything will be Happy Ever After."

At her words, the yells softened into mumbles. Apple smiled. But it wasn't a real smile. Could Headmaster Grimm really fix everything? When he ran off with the Storybook of Legends, Apple thought he'd looked afraid.

Daring was going on about how since he'd signed, his story was safe. But how could there be a story without an antagonist? Without the Evil Queen chasing her away, Snow White would never leave her castle for the forest, meet the dwarves, eat poisoned fruit, and wake to her prince.

And now Legacy Day was canceled for all of the rest of the students. The entire future of Ever After was uncertain. Apple just couldn't believe that Raven was capable of being so selfish.

Briar snorted and sat up, rubbing her eyes. "Was that all a bad dream?"

"No," said Duchess. "Everything is still a big, bad mess."

"I don't understand," said Blondie. "How could she? We've all dreamed and waited for this day for so long...."

Briar stood, stretching. "Well, Raven and her rebel friends may have destroyed our Legacy Day, but I refuse to let them ruin our Legacy Day dance. My planning committee worked too hard." She slid her crownglasses down from her head onto her nose. "We royals never abandon a party. We'll nobly see it through!"

CHAPTER 27

NOT YOUR MOMMA'S FAIRYTALE

RAVEN WAS ENJOYING THE SILENCE. Hundreds of audience members frozen, some on their feet, pointing at her, their faces in midshout. Others sitting back, confused. A few with expressions of surprise or even gratitude. And there was Maddie, smiling up at her.

Raven sent a yellow ray of magic, and Maddie moved.

"Wow!" said Maddie. "One of your spells finally worked properly!"

Raven felt an unexpected smile on her lips. "I know.... It feels good."

Maddie hopped up the steps and stood beside Raven, looking out at the wild statues of the audience.

"You were very brave today. I'm feeling so smart for choosing you to be my friend."

"Thanks, Maddie."

"Sooo...you gonna unfreeze everyone?"

"I guess I'll have to," said Raven. "Eventually. Things are going to get even crazier now, aren't they?"

"Sure as a pickle in a hat!" said Maddie. "But it'll work out. Stories always do. And you know which stories I like best? The new ones, the funny ones, the unexpected ones where I don't know what's going to happen next, but I can't wait to turn the page and find out."

"Yeah," said Raven. "Wouldn't it be awesome if our lives could be like those kinds of stories?"

Maddie gave Raven a hug.

And with that, Raven thought she was ready to face the consequences.

But with the unfreezing came the continued

shouting. So much shouting. And anger and fear. And it was all her fault. Was this what it felt like to be the Evil Queen?

No one seemed to notice when Raven cast a Dark Mist Spell. She meant to just try to sneak away. After all, Baba Yaga might be waiting nearby with a spray bottle. But naturally the spell backfired and sent Raven catapulting into the air. She screamed, feeling sympathy for Dexter's cabbages.

She seemed to go up, up, up for a long time, but the up part couldn't last forever. She was so high now, the crowd on the terrace was just a brown blur. Her rise slowed, then stopped. And then began the down part. Down, down, down—

Huge claws seized the silver collar of her cape. Wings beat as she rose.

"Nevermore, you scaly angel!" said Raven.

Nevermore cooed, sounding like a monstrous dove.

She hadn't signed. And yet Nevermore was still her pet. Didn't that mean something?

A school tower was incoming.

"Just drop me here," Raven said. If Headmaster Grimm came hunting for her, she wanted to be alone when found. She didn't want Nevermore to get in trouble, too.

Nevermore moaned but obeyed. Raven reached out and grasped the tower's banner pole. She scrambled onto the shingled roof and clung. No one would look for her there.

She waved good-bye to Nevermore. The dragon snuffled but flew back toward the forest, leaving Raven alone.

"What have I done?" Raven asked the wind. It beat the red banner that sprouted from the tower roof, but it didn't say anything helpful.

A bluebird landed on a shingle inches from Raven's hand, using its beak to scratch under its wing.

"Hi," Raven whispered.

The bluebird turned one eye to her. Raven held her breath. The bird chirped twice. Raven sang two notes in response. The bird didn't fly away.

"I changed things," she whispered. "It's already different."

Up here, Raven couldn't hear the screaming anymore. Maybe they'd all calmed down a bit, now that no one had actually *poofed*.

The wind was getting cold, the clouds stirred

up and gray. Raven climbed off the roof into the tower window and crept through hallways and down stairs. She didn't dare go back to her room. Apple might be there. Better to keep her distance for now.

Finally she ended up in the Commoner Common Room. She sat on a wooden stool by the fire and wondered how long she could hide before getting discovered.

Not long.

"See, there she is!" Maddie cried.

Suddenly Raven was smothered with hugs. Cedar, Maddie, Cerise, Hunter. Pink-haired Cupid flew in the door and attacked her in a huge and sincere embrace.

"You're okay!" said Cerise.

"We thought you *poofed*!" said Cedar. "I mean, you didn't sign the book and then you were gone, so naturally we thought…" Cedar's wooden brow furrowed. "I wish I could cry! I want to, but I'm not real enough. Curses!"

"I'm okay. Sorry to scare you. I just thought I'd better get out of there before the royals came after me with pitchforks and torches."

"I told everyone you didn't go *poof*, but they just looked at me funny," said Maddie.

Cedar shook her head. "You said, 'Tiny crow crowned unconfused with a cloud.'"

"Oh, whoops! Didn't realize I'd said it in Riddlish!" Maddie took off her hat and pulled out a cup of hot tea. "Here, Raven, I thought you could use this. On a cloudy day, there's nothing like milkflower tea with extra honey."

"Thanks," said Raven.

"Well, I thought what you did was amazing," said Cerise. "Raven Queen, what big guts you have!"

Everyone nodded.

Cerise took Raven's hand and looked at her intensely.

"Honestly," said Cerise. "Thank you for being brave enough."

Cerise's face was usually hidden in the shadow of her hood. Raven had never noticed before that she had a streak of white through her bangs and down the side of her straight dark hair. Raven thought her lightning forelock looked wicked cool.

There was a knock at the Common Room door. Hunter rushed to it.

"Who goes there?" Hunter demanded, his chest stuck out. "Be ye friend or foe?"

"Uh, friend, I think," came the voice. "I'm not completely sure what *foe* means, but probably not that one."

Hunter opened the door to Dexter.

"Hey," Dexter said.

Everyone took a protective stance in front of Raven. Dexter was clearly a royal, one of those promised a castle and a princess and a Happily Ever After. Those sort couldn't be happy with Raven right now.

"It's okay, guys," she said. "Dex is a friend."

Dexter took a couple of steps in. "I just wanted to make sure you were okay."

She nodded. "Thanks. I'm fine. But I'm sorry I messed up Legacy Day for everyone—for you especially. I know you wanted to see your Once Upon a Time."

Dexter shrugged, looking at her. And then he just kept looking at her, as if he'd forgotten that there was a roomful of people. He smiled. He didn't have his older brother's crowd-stopping, blinding smile, but Raven noticed just how nice a smile it was.

"You were amazing," Dexter said. "I've never... What you did... That was the bravest, the most extraordinary... I mean, you might have *poofed*! But you didn't!" He turned to Maddie. "Wasn't she amazing?"

Maddie nodded. "I heartily agree."

"Maybe it doesn't matter what future the book would have shown me. Maybe..." He looked back at his hands. "Maybe now everyone can choose for themselves without being afraid. Don't tell my brother, but I never liked the way things were, how you—how people were trapped in a story they didn't want to be in."

"Hear! Hear!" said Maddie. "After all, it's not everyone's destiny to run the best hat and tea shop in all of Ever After, and that's not fair!"

"I've been making this for you in Arts and Crafts," Cedar said, slipping a purple T-shirt into Raven's hand. Raven held it up. Cedar had embroidered a heart with wings in the center of the shirt flying over the words NOT YOUR MOMMA'S FAIRYTALE.

Raven put it on right over her clothes. She had to take off her crown and cape first, but she didn't mind.

"I should go," Dexter said. "Apple, Daring, and

the other royals will be leaving soon. Carriages are waiting to take us to the dock and the boats waiting to take us to the Ballroom. Briar is determined the Legacy Day dance should go forward."

"I'm pretty sure that I won't be welcome there," said Raven.

"Or your friends, either," said Cerise. "Except maybe Cedar, since she already signed."

"*Hmph*," said Cedar. "They'll just have to party without the puppet, 'cause I'm sticking with Raven."

"No, you should go," said Dexter. "You should all go. It's still Legacy Day. And you're still students at Ever After High. Don't let anyone bully you out of your party."

Raven smiled. "Okay, Dex. Maybe we will."

She looked around, and her smile felt a little bit wicked. But just a little bit.

They all raced down the many stairs to the courtyard of the school, just to see the carriages take off without them.

"We can still make it," said Dexter.

He led them on foot through the sports fields and down the lake-side hill to the shore. They arrived at the dock out of breath. The carriages had beat them by a long shot. Most of the royal-filled boats had already set off for the Ballroom, pulled by mermaids toward the lake island. Only one last boat was tied to the dock.

"Dexter!" Daring called, standing boldly in the rowboat as if it were a majestic royal vessel. "Get away from that rebel horde and come join the royals, where you belong."

Dexter hesitated.

"It's okay, Dex," said Raven. "We'll find a way to meet you there."

"There's room for them in here, too," Dexter said as he climbed in.

"Have you flipped your crown? It would be improper for them to attend a dance honoring Legacy Day. Raven Queen upset the ladies! Fair ones who have been looking forward to their Legacy Day since they were delicate little nursery rhymes. I've been wiping runny noses and catching fainting princesses all afternoon. So no dance for you, Raven Queen, or your friends. Finned one, proceed!" Daring called to a mermaid in the water.

She smiled up at Daring, batting her wet green eyelashes, and then grabbed the boat's rope and swam.

"Sorry!" Dexter called back.

The "Rebels" stood on the now empty dock.

"Um . . . I guess that's that," said Cerise.

"That?" said Maddie. "That is never that. This is that. Or else that is this. And this is definitely not *that*. So let's go to the dance."

"How?" said Raven.

CHAPTER 28

MADDIE ~~ANNOYS~~ Chats with THE NARRATOR ONE LAST TIME

Narrator? We're kind of stuck here on the shore. Any ideas?

Absolutely not. You know the rules.

Which rules? The rule about not putting things in your nose? Or the one about pretending to listen during Ancient History even if you're really thinking about how many cupcakes it would take to—

I've let myself get tricked into helping you too

often. I'm not supposed to take a side, you know—
Rebel *or* Royal. I'm supposed to tell both sides
equally, unbiased, some parts from Apple's point
of view, some parts from Raven's point of view. I
just report what happens according to how *they*
understand it, not tipping the story in favor of
one or the other, and certainly not giving hints
about how a group of Rebels might get to an island
without a boat. It seems impossible to me, anyhow.
I mean, you're not fish.

That's it! Thanks, Narrator!

But—I didn't say—I resent the idea that—*argh*!

CHAPTER 29

REWRITE, IGNITE, RESTART!

"I'VE GOT IT!" SAID MADDIE. "WE'RE NOT FISH. But *fish* are fish."

Maddie smiled proudly. Everyone else stared.

"Are you talking to *us* now or to that voice you sometimes hear?" asked Raven.

"To you, silly. We need fish to help us. Fishies in the water. Or things that can swim."

"Aah," said Raven. "That is a good idea. Besides the mermaids, who lives in this water?"

"I got this!" Cedar said, and jumped in. She was the school swim champ. After all, wood floats.

She swam out into the lake, her face down. She began to wave at something and talk underwater, the bubbles from her speech boiling around her face.

As she swam back to shore, a white wake formed behind her. Someone was following.

"What—" Cerise started.

"Wh-who—" Raven stuttered.

In the shallows, someone stood up. She had a young face, perhaps ten years old, and her skin was a pale blue. Her dark blue–black hair was long and flowed over her body. From the waist down she was underwater, but Raven suspected she didn't have feet.

"I've heard about you," the lake girl said to Raven. "I heard what you did today."

"Already? Wow. Gossip travels. Um, you're the daughter of the Sea Witch, aren't you?" said Raven. "One time your mom went to one of my mom's evil dinner parties."

The girl nodded. "I'm Coral Witch. Destined to one day live in the sea with a bunch of fat sea snakes as my pets and cut out a little mermaid's tongue to make a potion. Blech."

Raven leaned forward with her hand in a fist. "Potion-making-witch mom. Check."

Coral bumped her fist against Raven's.

"So, you guys want to get across?" Coral asked.

She put her face into the water and made noises. Suddenly the shore was swarming and bubbling with creatures: fish, eels, turtles, frogs, octopuses. They pressed together, forming a wet and lumpy surface.

"Hop on," said Coral.

The group held hands and carefully stepped onto the backs of the creatures, and the platform began to move. They wobbled, clinging to one another. Raven was not eager to fall onto the slimy surface. But the ride was surprisingly smooth. Soon they reached the island, and the teens stepped onto a wooden pier. The group shouted thanks to their lake friends.

Coral waved to them from the water. "Thank you! I'm going to think about what you did today, Raven."

The Ballroom, a white marble pavilion surrounded by carved pillars, sat atop the humpbacked island. Music floated down the slope, enticing Raven to follow. The group began to climb the steep stairs cut into the rocky cliff.

"You all sure you want to do this?" Raven asked.

"Do what?" said Maddie. "Go to a party? Of course we want to go to a party! What a silly question."

Cedar wrung out her cloak—a blush pink at the top that darkened into a black hem embellished with silver thread. "Nothing like crashing a party smelling like fish. Fitting, isn't it? Since I'll spend part of my story inside a whale." She looked up. "Or not. I mean, I don't know what will or won't happen anymore."

"I'm sorry," said Raven.

Cedar smiled, her wooden face creaking. "I like surprises."

Inside the Ballroom, the mood was somber. Sparrow Hood and his Merry Men played on the stage, slow songs that were too dismal to dance to. Clusters of Royals huddled together, some crying, some ranting. When Raven and her group entered, the conversations stopped. Everyone glared. Raven considered that the Royals had become professionally good glarers. Baba Yaga would be impressed.

"Apple." Raven sat beside her on a glass chair.

Apple's eyes were red from crying, but her cheeks were dry. "You're sorry."

Raven nodded.

"But you don't regret doing it," said Apple.

Raven nodded again.

Apple lifted her chin. "You don't need to be sorry for me, Raven Queen. I am sorry for you. I'll find a way to have my story. Maybe…maybe you'll change your mind and Headmaster Grimm can fix your page. Or maybe someone else can take your place as the Evil Queen. I *will* get my Happily Ever After. But you, Raven, you never will."

Apple walked away, surrounded by a crowd of friends. Every one of them looked back to glare again at Raven.

Raven felt everything at once—sad, hurt, angry, happy, hopeful, excited. A whole storybook of emotions battled inside her. She didn't know what to say, how to use this storm of energy. She wanted to dance hard. No, she wanted to sing.

Onstage, Sparrow Hood and his Merry Men were playing the Legacy Day anthem. Raven doubted whether that crew cared one way or another about signing the Storybook of Legends. But perhaps out of respect for the Royals, they sang the song low and slow, like a funeral march. Not a particularly great funeral march, either. The sound system screeched with feedback, and the music wailed like a lovesick cat.

Dexter joined her. "Hey," he said.

"I was never a fan of Legacy Day," said Raven, "but I've always loved this tune. At least, when it's sung well."

"Then sing it," said Dexter.

"Yes, yes, sing your song, Raven Queen," said Maddie. "Sing, sing, sing!"

"Okay," said Raven. It had become a day of unexpected choices for Raven. She'd never been on a stage before. But she jumped up there now, took a spare microphone, and started to sing along with Sparrow.

"Hey," he said. "Get off my stage."

Raven almost did. The stares from the crowd made her feel as if she were being pelted with pebbles and tomatoes. But she was singing, and for the first time in a long time, she felt all right with herself.

"Off!" Sparrow shouted. "*Get off!*"

The Merry Men's music faltered and stopped, but the drums kept going.

"Enough with the drums," said Sparrow.

"But she's got a wicked-bluesy voice, man." The drummer shrugged and kept playing a nice slow beat.

Sparrow blinked as if surprised one of his goons

would dare disobey him. He started toward the drummer, but Maddie shook her hat upside down on the stage. Out came the pig Snoof Piddle-dee-do. He snuffled at Sparrow's feet.

"Scat!" said Sparrow. "Shoo!"

The pig seemed to like the smell of Sparrow's green booties and chased him around the stage, trying to nibble the toes. Sparrow fled the attack, crashing into the cymbals, knocking over an amp, and finally running offstage.

The guitarists and bassist shrugged, too, and started to play along with the drummer, and Raven sang the Legacy Day song.

> *Believe that everything is waiting for you.*
> *Accept that your life is set in stone.*
> *It's time to take your promised tale*
> *and become the person you've always known.*

But the words no longer felt true to Raven. She looked back at the drummer and, smiling, snapped her fingers in a faster rhythm. He fell into a rock-and-roll beat. The guitarist and bassist laid into their instruments. And the Merry Men rocked it like

Rockabye Baby's cradle. This bough was about to break.

Raven bobbed her head. She took center stage. And she changed the words.

> *It's an open book, a road in reverse,*
> *a brand-new hook—forget that curse.*
> *It's a rebel cause with a royal heart.*
> *Rewrite, ignite, restart.*

A few people in the crowd sang back, "*Rewrite, ignite, restart!*"

"Yeah!" said Raven into the microphone. She put her fist in the air, for the first time in her life unafraid. "Rewrite, ignite, restart, Ever After High!"

Some of the crowd cheered.

Raven kept on singing.

Soon, half the room was singing with her, including Maddie, Hunter, Cedar, Cerise, Kitty, and Cupid. Did she see Dexter Charming bobbing his head? Good old Dexter. But his brother Daring was glaring at Raven as if he could shoot arrows with his eyes. And maybe he could. She'd seen him swordfight holding the sword with his feet. And win.

Briar, Ashlynn, and the other princesses stood by, watching but not singing. Briar couldn't help nodding to the beat. The girl loved a good dance tune. Regret still stung Ashlynn's eyes. Behind Briar's back, she reached out. From nearby, Hunter reached forward, and in the shadows they held hands.

Raven's beautiful, perfect roommate, Apple, looked like she would shrivel up and cry. But then her chin stuck out, her shoulders went back, her head raised. Apple's determined expression gave Raven mother-goosebumps. This wasn't over. Apple hadn't given up on Raven or their story.

Raven felt that pit in her stomach roll around and threaten to grow into a beanstalk of guilt. Maybe she'd destroyed Apple's story. But even more she hoped that now *everyone* might have a chance at an unexpected, unwritten, unsung story that would be, as Blondie would say, just right.

Raven kept singing. The future was as uncertain as a Wonderlandian riddle. But for Raven, at least, the Legacy Day dance was Happily Ever After.

Mysterious EPILOGUE

"SHE DOESN'T KNOW WHAT SHE'S DOING," Milton Grimm muttered as he fled the ruined Legacy Day ceremony. "She doesn't know what she's done!"

The faculty was in chaos, chasing after the headmaster with questions and shouts of concern. Mr. Badwolf howled. Counselor Mother Goose clucked. Coach Gingerbreadman was especially speedy. But Grimm managed to get to his office first and lock the door. He leaned against it, still cradling the Storybook of Legends in his arms. In the hallway, he could hear Baba Yaga cackling.

"How dare Raven Queen defy me?" he whispered. "How dare that girl question Milton Grimm?"

He carefully opened the book and touched the torn remains of Raven Queen's page. He shuddered, as if touching a wound.

He put the book safely back into its case and locked it tight. And then he began to pace.

How could everything have gone so wrong? He'd been meticulous! Using an eavesdropping spell, he'd overheard Raven and Dexter in the library after the Legacy Day practice. She wanted to hunt down Old Man Winters. Well, by the time she reached Book End, Grimm had been ready. Dressed in a perfect Illusion Spell, he'd sat in the park feeding the pigeons, so they'd see him first before going to the real Old Man Winters's house.

Grimm had slipped that sketchbook into Bella Sister's box in the Lost and Crowned Office. He'd made sure that Raven and Apple saw the trollskin tree in the Enchanted Forest. And the Crumbling Spell on the fake letter couldn't have worked better! Had the quest to the caves gone too far? He didn't think so. After that long and dangerous journey, he was certain Raven would be exhausted, discouraged by the skeleton, and convinced by those fateful words he'd sent Helga and Gus to paint on the cave wall.

No, his plan had been a brilliant balance between mysterious and obvious. Something else must have happened to make Raven question his fake story. Someone else must have—

From far away, Grimm heard the sound of knocking.

Giles? Had Raven found Giles? His troublesome brother did have dangerous ideas about allowing choice to replace destiny. But no, that was impossible. No one knew how to enter the Vault of Lost Tales. Giles was safely locked away where he could do no more harm.

Grimm seized a pitcher of water and threw it across his office. It shattered against the tile floor. How could he have failed?

Well, it wasn't over. He straightened his tie and smoothed back his hair. He would find a way to get Raven to sign. He would cure the school of this "choice" madness and restore tradition and safety to Ever After.

"I am Milton Grimm!" he whispered. "My word is law. And those who break it will pay!"

From deep within his office he heard a cackle. How had Baba Yaga gotten in?

Grimm followed the sound. No sign of the old sorceress. But a faint glow crept out of the mirror he used for Mirrorcasts. From inside the mirror, the cackle built to a deep, throaty laugh.

ACKNOWLEDGMENTS

Every book requires a team of people to bring it into creation, but this one more than most. The enchanting team at Mattel built the world of Ever After and all its fabulous characters. Fairy kisses to Cindy Ledermann, Lara Dalian, Emily Kelly, Christine Kim, Robert Rudman, and Ira Singerman. Thanks for letting me play in your playground!

Thanks to the royally rebellious team at Little, Brown, including Erin Stein, Connie Hsu, Andrew Smith, and Melanie Chang.

Dean, Max, and Maggie Hale are not only a fine crew of lovable misfits but also charming collaborators. Thanks for your wisdom, patience, and hexcellent humor.

Turn the page for a sneak peak of
The Legend of Shadow High

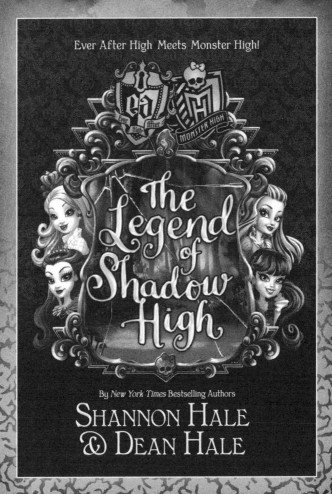

Ever After High Meets Monster High!

The Legend of Shadow High

By *New York Times* Bestselling Authors

SHANNON HALE
& DEAN HALE

CHAPTER 1

IT'S MORNING AT MONSTER HIGH. THE OLD building sits up on Monster Hill like...like... uh, I'm trying to think of a good simile here. I studied similes last semester, but I'm still new at narrating. It sat on the hill like a big, dark birthday cake? Like a hairless rock giant? Like a fancy pointed hat worn by particularly well-behaved geographical features?

Ugh, I'm already messing this up! I'm not supposed to say *I*, for starters. *I* am the Narrator, not a character in this story. Let me start over.[1]

---

1 *Psst.* Hey, Reader. Yeah, you. Hi, I'm Brooke Page, the Narrator for this story! Since it's against Narrator Rules for me to talk directly to you, when I need to tell you something, I'll just whisper it down here in the footnotes, okay? I hope that's not boldly against the rules.

Ahem. It's morning at Monster High. The spiders are humming, the termites are chittering, the wind is sliding through the shutters with an eerie whistle. A beautiful day.

Oh, and hey! There are Draculaura and Frankie Stein! Walking through the massive front doors, carrying their bags on their shoulders, with absolutely no idea of the epic, possibly world-ending story that's about to unravel.

Draculaura is a vampire—obviously. Pale pink skin, long fangs, glossy black hair with pink highlights, a pink-and-black dress with polka dots. Frankie has mint-green skin and black hair shocked with thick white stripes. You can see the seams in her arms and legs where her father, Frankenstein, stitched her together.

Both girls are super excited. You can tell by the way they're walking—a hop in their step, nearly skipping. But Frankie is also nervous. You can tell from that shiver in her hands and tremor in her chin.[2]

"Don't forget the intro music," says Draculaura.

"I've got it queued up on my iCoffin," Frankie

---

2 Plus, I can guess their thoughts. Well, at the moment, just Frankie's, so that's why she's the point-of-view character in this chapter. It's a Narrator thing.

says, holding up her coffin-shaped phone as they pass the coffin-shaped lockers.[3] "Have you got the—"

"Sound effects?" says Draculaura, pulling a portable keyboard from her pack. "Check!"

"And the—"

"Images?" says Draculaura. "The photo slide show is totes on my iCoffin."

"Right. But don't forget the special effects," says Frankie, handing Draculaura the Portable EffecTacular that Frankie made in her lab. The size of a toaster, it creates all sorts of monstrous effects.

"Are you sure we should use the EffecTacular?" asks Draculaura. "The other students won't have smoke clouds and ice storms in their presentations. I didn't have much time to practice with it and"—Draculaura plays with the hem of her skirt—"it seems kinda…umm…scary…but not in a good way?"

"Well, maybe we don't *need* them," says Frankie, "but they'll make our presentation voltageous."

---

3 Coffins: It's a monster thing.

"Well, of course! But getting back to the dangerous part…Um, maybe our presentation will still be great even without the EffecTacular?"

"Great?" Frankie's neck bolts buzz with excitement. "But great isn't enough. Not near enough. We're the cofounders of Monster High. They're going to expect something…something *amazing*!"

"Oh, okay, I'm sure you're right."

Today their history class will give their oral presentations on the creation of Monster High. And since Frankie and Draculaura kinda, sorta actually founded the school, Frankie feels a wee bit of pressure to kinda, sorta actually be *spooktacular*.[4]

They slide into their seats just as Mr. Rotter starts the class.

"Let's see," he says, rubbing his fingers over his pallid gray forehead, "I believe Marshall is up first."

The small swamp monster slurps his way to the front of the class, blinks his one eye, and shrugs

---

4 I, for one, am still geeking out about getting to narrate a story about *the* Frankie Stein and *the* Draculaura! I'm a huge fan, but don't tell them. I'm trying to play it cool.

the tangled knot of his thorny vine hair out of the way.

"So…" says Marshall. "I, uh, lived in a swamp. I ate swamp stuff, you know? Did swamp things. Then Frankie and Drac found me and said, 'Hey, we started a school called Monster High and, hey, you should come and learn stuff and not be alone all the time.' So I did."

Marshall sits back down.

"Thank you, Marshall," says Mr. Rotter, lids blinking slowly over his black eyes. "Next time work on details and listing references, okay? Well, I hope Draculaura and Frankie will be an example to you all of a proper oral presentation."

"You bet we will!" Draculaura says.

She smiles at Frankie, her fangs glinting.

Frankie smiles back.

No pressure, no pressure, Frankie tells herself. *Just be amazing. How hard can it be to be amazing?*

Frankie joins Draculaura in front of the class and gulps. So many eyes look back! Some blue, some green, some black, some bulging, some wiggling on the ends of tentacles. All staring. At her.

Moving to Monster High and making so many friends has been Frankie's fondest scream come true. But sometimes she still feels like the lonely ghoul hidden inside her father's laboratory.

From the back row, her ghoulfriend Clawdeen Wolf gives her a claws-up and a toothy smile.[5]

Frankie returns the thumbs-up, relieved that her hand doesn't take it as an invitation to wander off in that direction...without the rest of her. She clears her throat. No time for nerves—Draculaura is depending on her!

"So. Um. Once upon a time..." Frankie starts.

The class giggles. *Once upon a time* is how fairytales start, and monsters definitely don't believe in fairytales.

Their laughs give Frankie more confidence, a sign that she's being entertaining, at least. "Once upon a time," she says, pressing PLAY on her iCoffin. Mysterious music fills the room. "There was a vampire named Draculaura...."

Draculaura presses the first button on the EffecTacular—FRANKIE'S MIST POTION. A cloud of

5 Clawdeen: daughter of werewolves. Seriously cool ghoul.

smoke billows out of the little machine. Through it walks Draculaura, dramatic, her hands up.

"Ta-da!" she says.

The students clap. A few, the ones who don't enjoy breathing a little swamp gas, cough on the smoke.

"Uh, sorry," says Frankie, fanning it away.

She begins to tell the tale of how Draculaura lived with her father, Dracula, in a big, ancient house on a hill for many, many years till the night she went out flying in bat form and first met Frankie. They both had been longing for a life like the Normie teenagers had: attending high school, fanging out with friends, just living in the open. So they started to search for other monsters like them who'd been hiding from the Normies.[6] Monsters who were aching for a different kind of life.

"First we went to the swamps," says Frankie. "There had to be monsters there, right?"

"Right!" says Marshall from his seat.

---

6 In case you don't know, Normies are what the monsters call normal people (i.e., not monsters). Monster history has shown that whenever Normies know monsters are real and might, for instance, be living on a hilltop close to their town, they flip out, and things tend to go very badly for the monsters. So, long ago, the monster community decided that hiding from the Normies was the best solution.

"And so, one Tuesday night…" says Frankie.

Draculaura plays a creepy sound effect on her keyboard and presses the WET FROG SMELL button on the EffecTacular. A panel slides open, revealing a small, wet frog. An equally small fan begins to whir behind the frog, blowing its humid smell out to the class. But right then, Frankie's iCoffin battery runs out and the music stops. She touches her finger to it to jolt it with electricity. Oops. A bright spark leaps from the iCoffin, through the moist air, and into the EffecTacular. Turns out homemade special effects machines do not handle surprise electricity very well. All the little hatches of the device open at once, and its living contents—including the tiny frog, a swarm of pyramid moths, and one very excited scorpion—make an escape.

The class screams. The scorpion trots across Mr. Rotter's desk and begins to happily sting the stacks of paper.

"Loose beasts!" yells Frankie. "Drac, get the scorpion bag!"

"I got it," says Draculaura, pulling out a canvas bag labeled SCORPIONS. Oh no, Frankie must have brought the wrong bag. Instead of being a nice, empty place to put an escaped scorpion, it is full of *extra* scorpions, which scuttle out and scamper toward the students. More screams. Students run, crawl, and slither through the door.[7]

"Sorry!" yells Frankie as she chases the leaping frog. "We have to slow them down! Try the…uh…. the SIMULATED ICY NORTH button on the EffecTacular!"

"Is it still working?"

"Here, let me," says Frankie, taking the EffecTacular from Draculaura. She aims it at the scorpion on the desk and presses the button just as Mr. Rotter runs toward it with the classroom pyre extinguisher. The Icy North spray hits the extinguisher, which pops like a balloon filled with liquid ice.

"No!" the girls scream.

Mr. Rotter is frozen in a block of ice from the neck down. He tries to take a step, but he tips and falls face-first with a *thud*.

"Ow," he says, his mouth pressed against the floor. A scorpion scampers over him and out the door.

---

7 Like, literally *through* the door. Usually, monsters remember to open doors first. Usually.

"Sorry," says Frankie. "Sorry? Um, really, really sorry."

The classroom is empty, a swamp monster–shaped hole in the door. Just Clawdeen remains, capturing the last scorpion and stuffing it into her backpack for safekeeping.

Mr. Rotter mumbles something incoherent from the floor.

Frankie clears her throat. "Um, Mr. Rotter? Is this a good time to show you our big finale?"

Later, Frankie and Draculaura are in their room, slumped on their beds.[8] Their clothes smell like smoke. Their shoes are wet from melted ice.

"We have only two days," Frankie mutters.

"Yep," Draculaura mutters.

"It took us a *week* to get ready for this report," Frankie mutters.

"Yep," Draculaura mutters, continuing the whole muttering trend.

---

8 If you wonder why we skipped ahead, it's because I had to grab a snack. Now you know: When you're reading a book and time jumps forward, the reason is probably that the Narrator had to take a break or, like, go to bed or something.

They are too despondent to do anything besides slump on their beds and mutter. Mr. Rotter has given them forty-eight hours to come up with a new oral report on a high school—but it can't be on Monster High, because, he said, "apparently your Monster High reports include frostbite and scorpion assault."

"I'm so sorry, Drac," says Frankie. "I don't know why I packed extra scorpions. I was just worried something would go wrong, and…and I should've let you do the ice one—"

Draculaura giggles a little. "Now that it's over? Mr. Rotter as a giant ice pop was top ten–level funny."

Frankie laughs. Then sighs. "I just wanted it to be really amazing. I guess we'll have to do our report on—"

"Normie High," Draculaura finishes. "It's the only other high school I know anything about. But we can't go down to the village to research it in person. My dad would flip his coffin if we went anywhere near the Normies."

"Besides, everyone already knows about Normies," says Frankie. "We need to do something different to make up for that…that *monstrous* disaster."

Draculaura perks up. "Come on," she says, taking Frankie's hand. She gets to the door of the room before she realizes Frankie isn't attached to her hand.[9]

"Wait for the rest of me!" says Frankie, jogging after her. She sews her hand back to her wrist while they run into the principal's[10] office, which contains his massive personal library.

"Dad always says, 'Anything you need you can find in a book,'" says Draculaura.

"What if I need a cheese sandwich?" Frankie whispers. Her stomach rumbles with hunger. In all her excitement for their presentation, Frankie forgot to eat breakfast. Draculaura grabs an apple off the desk and tosses it across the room. Frankie catches it and takes a bite while examining the shelves.

Soon she's absorbed in reading gold-lettered spines and searching tables of contents for anything about high school.

"Hey," says Frankie. "This book says that ages ago, before monsters went into hiding, there was another school for monsters, so this isn't the first Monster High!"

9 Don't be alarmed, Reader. Limbs coming loose is a thing that happens to Frankie.
10 Dracula is the principal of the school. How fangtastic is that?

It would make a fangtastic report…if only Mr. Rotter hadn't forbidden them from presenting on Monster High again.

"Look at this!" says Drac.

What she's holding can hardly be called a book. It's just a bundle of papers sewn together with waxed thread, the parchment so old it's turned brown. Written in smudged watery ink on the front are the words *Shadow High*.[11]

Frankie reads the title out loud and then rubs her arms. "I didn't know I was physically capable of getting goosebumps, but I just did."

"Me too," says Draculaura. "There's something about that name…*Shadow High*…."

Frankie flips through the pages, but they're blank.

"Why would your dad have a blank book? Is it a diary no one ever used?"

"It's totes old," says Drac. "Maybe the ink faded."

"I dunno," says Frankie, peering at the pages.

---

11 Oh no. Here we go. I can feel it. This is where the real plot starts. The reason no other Narrators will touch this story. I'd warn the girls, but even if interfering with the characters weren't hugely against Narrator Rules, they can't hear me. Only you, Reader, know what I narrate. Oh, and also a couple of very unique characters, whom I have a feeling we'll meet soon.

"Looks to me like someone erased it. On purpose. And there I go, getting goosebumps again."

They run to find Dracula, who is having a cup of tea with Clawdeen's mom on the veranda, overlooking the cemetery.

"Shadow High? I've never heard of it." Dracula rubs his arms. "*Ooh*, did the temperature just drop? I'm suddenly chilly. And I thought I was already the *coolest* dad ever."[12]

He laughs heartily. Clawdeen's mom joins in.

"I mean... there is a *bite* in the air," he says, smiling with his fangs showing. The two adults laugh again.

Draculaura rolls her eyes. "Yeah... funny, Dad. But anyhoo, about Shadow High?"

"Hmm... Shadow High... You say you found it in *my* library? You know, I think I used to know—"

Dracula is interrupted by a distant plopping noise.

"What was that sound?" he says.

"Oh dear," says Clawdeen's mom. "I hope the pipes aren't leaking."

They both get up and go to check.

---

12 Dad jokes, amirite? They seem to be universal, no matter whether the dad is vampire or Normie or Narrator.

The girls look at each other. Draculaura sighs.

"Dad jokes, amirite?" she says.[13]

The girls rush back down, nearly tackling Mr. Mum-Ho-Tep, who is sweeping the floor at the base of the stairs. Mr. Mum-Ho-Tep is so old he's worn down to almost nothing. His hair under his janitor cap billows around him, thinner than cobwebs, and his skin is like paper. When he exhales, he nearly disappears when viewed from the side. Frankie reasons that anyone who's lived that long must have heard of everything, even—

"Shadow High?" he whispers in response to her question. "That name sounds familiar. Let me think...."

He taps his temple in concentration, but just then a *plop* noise sounds from...somewhere.

"What was that plop?" he asks in his raspy voice. "It broke my concentration."

"I don't know," says Draculaura. She smiles sweetly. "Now, you were saying—"

"About Shadow High?" Frankie prompts.

"Ah, yes. Shadow High. That name is ominous,

---

13 Omigosh, that's exactly what I said a minute ago! I bet me and Drac would be friends if she knew I existed!

isn't it? I'd bet my very last toenail I've heard it before.... It's on the edge of my memory, or in a memory that has somehow been erased from my mind. But if I concentrate..." He closes his eyes.

Plop. Plop.

"Upside-down pyramids!" he exclaims. "What in the ancient world is that plopping sound? I have to find it!"

And off he goes, on the hunt for the plop.[14]

Frankie rubs her arms. They're speckled with—you guessed it—goosebumps.

"Does it almost seem like—" Draculaura starts.

"There's a random plopping noise whenever—" Frankie continues.

"We ask someone about..." Draculaura pauses, then whispers, "*Shadow High?*"

Frankie nods. "It's so mysterious! We have to get to the bottom of this."

"Are you sure we should?" says Draculaura. "Doesn't something about it seem...creepy?"

Frankie hesitates. First the goosebumps, and now she feels as if there are skeleton moths in her stomach.

---

14 Wait a sentence! What are all these plops? I'm as confused as you are, Reader.

She pulls her shirt up an inch, and through a seam in her waist a moth crawls out and flits away.

"But don't you think that this *Shadow High*"—she whispers the name—"might be the perfect subject for our report? Like it was just waiting for us to discover it!"

"You're right!" says Draculaura, straightening. "We're monsters. Things are supposed to be scared of *us*, not the other way around!"

Frankie nods. She can tell Draculaura is a little scared but pushing through it. Frankie is proud she's the BGF[15] of such a courageous monster. She stands up straighter while hopeful zaps of electricity travel up her spine.

"Shadow High does sound creepy-cool, doesn't it?" Frankie says. "Maybe it's some other, secret Monster High!"

Plop. Plop.

"Did you hear that plop?" asks Draculaura.

"Never mind the plop. I've got an idea."

---

15 BGF: Best Ghoulfriend Forever.

CHAPTER 2

Mom. Dad. I know it was you interrupting my narration with that plopping sound. Are you following me around? Where are you? Aha! Mom, I can see you hiding behind those vines and dangling participles.

Brooke, sweetie…

You too, Dad. Come out from behind the spoiler tree. Honestly, you're a terrible hider. I can totally see your shoes.

Brooke, honey …

Hey, what's that thing you're holding? A vacuum or something?

No. It's ... well, it's a Plop Device.

You mean a *plot* device? I learned about that. It's anything that helps move the story forward. Like, the temperature of the Three Bears' porridge is a plot device because it causes the bears to leave to let it cool, and then their absence makes it possible for Goldilocks to break in—

Yes, yes, you're very smart, Brooke, but this is ... ahem, it's not a plot device. It's a Plop Device.

I've never heard of it.

Yeah ... it's top secret. The characters in a story can't hear us speaking,[16] *but they can hear the sounds this machine makes. Narrators aren't supposed to interfere in any way, of course—*

But a plopping noise is such a small interference.

Yes, exactly. Sometimes a well-timed plopping noise can distract a character who is about to do something that might ruin the story.

Are you trying to distract the characters? Or stop the story from happening altogether? But why? What

---

16 Except for a couple of them, whom you'll meet soon!

is it that you don't want Frankie and Draculaura to discover? What is Shadow High?

Shhh! Don't even say those words. And please stop narrating! I don't want you anywhere near this story. It's too dangerous.

I don't get why you and the other Narrators don't want this story to be told. Draculaura and Frankie will do whatever they're going to do whether we narrate it or not.

But, Brooke—

Maybe I'm just a kid, but I know that every story deserves to be told. And if no one narrates this one, then the Readers will never know what happens! So if you won't do it, I will.

CHAPTER 3

Frankie Stein lived all her early life in a laboratory: covered windows; nice, clean concrete floors; flickering lights; and the comforting buzz of electricity. Endless books to read, gadgets to fiddle with, and contraptions to invent—like that electric flyswatter she wired up, or the automatic spoon...which more often than not missed her mouth and spooned cereal into her ear.

So it was mostly good! But also, it was *so* lonely.

Unlike all Normie kids and most monsters, Frankie wasn't born a baby who grew up into a teenager. She was *created* as a teenager. She woke up one day on a slab and had to figure out what *teenager* even meant. Frankie used to scour the Monster Web for information about Normie teenagers, peer through the slats of a lab window, and wish for friends who could understand just how creepy-cool life was.

And now at last she has those longed-for friends, especially her BGF, Draculaura. Far worse than having to go back into hiding again would be disappointing her friends. She's certain she let down Drac with the presentation. So what's a ghoul to do? Fix it!

In their bedroom, Frankie grabs the Mapalogue[17] from the closet and places the box on her desk.

"The Mapalogue? To find Shadow High?" says Draculaura. "That only works to locate monsters."

"Yeah, but what if Shadow High *is* monsters?" says Frankie. "It kinda sounds like it."

She opens the box, and the wooden map unfolds. It's smooth, polished by the fingers, claws, and tentacles of all the monsters who have used it over the centuries to find one another in a world full of Normies.

17 The Monster Mapalogue is like a monster detector, complete with a world map and a Skullette magical teleporting thingamabob.

Burned into the wood's surface are the borders and names of all the known places of the world.

The Mapalogue was how Frankie and Drac had found monsters hiding in various locations and then transported themselves there to deliver an invitation to Monster High. When they touched the Skullette token Draculaura now wore around her neck and spoke the words *Exsto monstrum* plus the monster's name, the Mapalogue could send them directly to that monster. It was how they found Cleo de Nile, daughter of the Mummy, hidden in her royal tomb home beneath the desert sands. And how they found Lagoona Blue, daughter of the sea monster, emerging from the surf to meet them beachside.

"The problem is we don't know anyone's name at Shadow High," says Draculaura.

"It's a school, right?" says Frankie. "There's got to be a principal."

Frankie shivers with excitement. Or maybe a jolt of all that loose electricity just surged through her body and bolted up her spine. Either way, it is clawesome having friends. Friends mean adventures in a world so much bigger than a boarded-up laboratory.

Frankie takes her friend's hand. Draculaura touches

the Skullette pendant around her neck. They take a breath. And then—

Plop. Plop.

"What the…?"

"Seriously, what is that plopping sound?" says Draculaura.

"Let's just ignore it."

They hold hands again, touch the Skullette, look at the map, and together say, *"Exsto monstrum principal of Shadow High—"*

And they fall. But not out of Monster High and into Shadow High. Just onto their butts. On their bedroom floor. Not transported. They were knocked down by nothing.

"What just—"

"Did that—"

Their door swings open. Clawdeen pushes her voluminous brown hair out of her eyes.

"Ghouls, did you feel that?" says Clawdeen. "I think we just had an earthquake! I'm gonna go check on my little brothers."

And she bounds off just as quickly as she entered.

"That was—" Frankie starts.

"Creepy," Draculaura finishes.

They stand up, brush themselves off, and shrug. They aren't hurt. So they try it again. Hands held. Skullette touched. Deep breaths. As they speak, the plopping sounds return.[18]

"Exsto monstrum"—plop, plop—*"principal"*—PLOP— *"of Shadow"*—plopplopplopplopplop—*"High!"*

Almost before the words come out of their mouths, another tremor rolls beneath their feet. The stones of Monster High groan, the wood floor buckles, the books on their shelves burst off like popping corn. And most ominously, the mirror on the wall cracks in two. Now Frankie is shivering for real. Two earthquakes in a row? That can't be a coincidence—

"Whoa!" exclaims Draculaura.

"What?" says Frankie.

"Look!"

"Look at what?"

"Whoa! Look! Whoa!"

Draculaura finally points at the map. Frankie gasps.

"How…how did…but how did…" Frankie mumbles.

---

18 Honestly. My parents can be so weird sometimes.

"I have no idea," Draculaura whispers.

The map, which was burned into the wood who knew how many centuries or even millennia ago, has changed. It's as if it has zoomed out and revealed that the places they know are only one small part of all the world. The map of their world is squished down in the corner. And new lands with new borders are burning into the wood right before their eyes. One particularly large continent-like part bears a name: EVER AFTER HIGH.

ABOUT THE AUTHOR

New York Times bestselling author SHANNON HALE knew at age ten that it was her destiny to become a writer. She has quested deep into fairy tales in such enchanting books as *The Goose Girl*, *Book of a Thousand Days*, *Rapunzel's Revenge*, and Newbery Honor recipient *Princess Academy*. With the princely and valiant writer Dean Hale, Shannon coauthored four charming children, who are free to follow their own destinies. Just so long as they get to bed on time.